Jane's Journal

Book 8 in Clover Creek Caravan

Kirsten Osbourne

Chapter One

Sunday, July 11th, 1852

I am so thankful we have found the place where we will settle. We hope to make the journey back by mid-October. Buildings must go up in a hurry, but I will probably be teaching the children who are on this journey with us. It will be a good way for me to support my unborn child. The dream was for Adam to ranch out here, and we'd build a real home where we could watch our children grow up. I miss Adam so much, but I think I miss the lost dream even more.

While we're camped here in Clover Creek, my future home, I will be helping Mr. Henderson and his children. Mrs. Henderson was the first fatality of our journey, and now he's got a badly sprained ankle. His children will still need to eat, so I will offer to take over his campfire. He may not want or need the help, but his children look as if they haven't had a decent meal since their mother died. If I do nothing else, I can rectify that.

After our church services, Katie Bedwell and I will make pies, and if Katie is willing, I will take a pie to Mr. Henderson and offer to do what I can. I hope he's still able to drive, because I don't think the captains would be willing to stop for him. When someone dies in the company, we bury them right on the trail, and then the wagons roll over their burial site, in hopes they'll pack the dirt enough and disguise the scent, and the wolves won't dig them up. I can't imagine a group of people who does that would stop for a sprained ankle.

I often hear wolves at night. I didn't before Adam died, because I knew he would protect me from anything, but now that he's passed, it's all I hear while I try to sleep. Of course, I'm so tired from being pregnant and walking twenty miles a day that I'm thankfully able to sleep each night. I do feel as if God is watching over me.

We'll leave early tomorrow morning to continue our journey toward Oregon City. I wish we could just stay here and claim the land the way our ancestors did here in America, but I know that's not possible. The government needs us to file a document saying that we are going to homestead the land. Or in my case, I will homestead the land. Adam is no longer with me, no matter how many times I expect him to just walk toward me at the end of the day.

I must send a letter to my mother when we go through a town or fort again. I've written to tell her of Adam's death, but I haven't gotten to a place where I can mail it to her yet. I will do that at the first possible occasion.

After Jane Davies finished making pies with Katie Bedwell that afternoon, Jane carried one of the pies to the Henderson family. They occasionally took meals with Margaret and her family, but they didn't have a great deal of money, and now that Mr. Henderson couldn't hunt to pay for his portion of the meal, it would be better if someone made the Henderson family their personal project. Jane was certain it would help her to keep going as well. It was hard to know she was having a fatherless baby in a matter of months.

Jane's long dark hair was pulled into a bun at the back of her neck. She could feel some tendrils escaping both onto her forehead and at the nape of her neck. She was going to have to let out her yellow "good" dress soon as her burgeoning belly outgrew it.

When Jane reached the Hendersons' camp, she spotted Mr. Henderson on the ground, looking defeated. His hair was a little longer than it should be, and she could tell he hadn't shaven his blond beard in quite some time. Jane understood completely. They'd already come so many miles from home, and it was too late to turn back. But he was hurt, his children were hungry, and his wife had passed months before.

"Excuse me, Mr. Henderson," Jane said softly. "Katie Bedwell and I baked pies today, and I thought perhaps you and your family would enjoy one."

Mr. Henderson looked up at Mrs. Davies in surprise. He didn't think they'd ever spoken. "That would be most welcome, Mrs. Davies. How are you doing without Adam? He and I were on watch together several times. He was a good man."

Jane smiled and took a deep breath. "I'm plodding along like everyone else is." The babe she carried was all that kept her going, but it would be indelicate to mention her condition to a man she was unrelated to.

"I understand. When I lost my wife, I was certain the earth would open up and swallow me whole. I must keep going for my children," he said, grimacing at his foot the doctor had wrapped to stabilize.

"Yes, you must. Who will drive your wagon now that you're no longer able?"

He laughed softly. "I'll keep driving my wagon. I just wish I had someone cooking for my youngsters. I seem to only be able to cook beans, and they are getting mighty tired of beans."

Jane smiled. "That's part of the reason I came to talk to you. It's hard for me to just keep pushing on without Adam, but if I could be allowed to cook for you and the children—at least until you're better if not for the entire trip—I think I'd have a reason to get up each morning that has nothing to do with our final destination."

Mr. Henderson closed his eyes for a moment. "You're an answer to prayers. We would welcome your help. I can't pay you, but I'll help build you a house once we're settled."

"That would be more than enough payment. I'll make sure the children keep up as well. I was a schoolteacher back in Wisconsin, and I would dearly love to help with them."

"I would be forever thankful for your help if you really don't mind."

"Not at all. As I said, it'll be good for me." Jane looked at the small campfire. "May I use your food and some of my own to prepare meals?"

"Absolutely. I don't suppose you're willing to start cooking for us tonight? My little ones have only had berries to eat so far today."

Jane's eyes widened. She hadn't realized it was quite as bad as it was. "I'll start now. I have some venison the hunters brought in last night. Perhaps I could make a meal from that and some rice?"

He nodded. "That would be wonderful. Anything to fill us up. We'd be happy with Johnny cakes for supper."

"Why don't I do Johnny cakes now? It's late for the noon meal, but that's no reason to let your children go hungry. I'll make them now, and I'll do the venison meal around supper time. Some of the other women have made certain that I get a share of whatever meat is shot. It won't be a lot once we stretch it, but it'll be better than nothing."

"I would be obliged. Thank you for your generosity."

Jane had a new spark in her step as she headed back toward Katie's camp. She was certain she could talk the other woman out of another small portion of meat to feed the Henderson family.

As soon as she mentioned the children hadn't eaten yet that day, Katie cut off a large chunk of meat, and then she offered to come help cook. "I'm not needed at the moment."

Jane shook her head. "No, I can do it. Thanks for reminding me how good it feels to help others, even when you feel like you want to die yourself."

Katie sighed. "This terrible journey has done it to us all. I just pray life really is better when we get settled."

Jane took the venison over to the Henderson camp and then started digging through the back of their wagon for cornmeal. She found a jug of honey as well as the cornmeal, so pulled that out as well, thinking the children may enjoy the honey on their Johnny cakes.

Mr. Henderson watched her as she cooked, as if he was trying to memorize everything she did. "I never much cared about what happened in the kitchen as long as what was going on ended in a delicious meal for me. I should have learned from Judy."

"You had no way of knowing this would happen. The Trail is hard, but I think the end is worth it. Having all that free land. What do you plan to do with your free land, Mr. Henderson?" Jane asked.

"The original plan was to build a small hotel, where Judy would cook for the guests. Now I think the plan is to be a farmer or rancher. I didn't really bring enough livestock to be a rancher though. Perhaps there will be a place I can get some. I did bring three female oxen and a male. I'm not sure I can base an entire herd on that, though."

Jane frowned. "Do you want to be a farmer?"

He shrugged. "My father is a farmer back in Kentucky. I always thought I'd follow in his footsteps, but Judy had grand ideas."

"You could still start a small hotel if you had someone helping you, couldn't you?"

Mr. Henderson sighed. "Well, sure, but who would want to cook for me? Even ask my children how bad my beans always turn out."

"It may be something I'm interested in. I thought I was coming west to be a ranch wife, and we do have plenty of livestock, just no man to build a house and build fences. I could also be persuaded to not teach all day and cook for you instead. That would make it easier to take care of my baby."

He frowned for a moment, and then his eyes widened. "A baby, huh? That's going to be hard with no man to support you."

"Trust me," she said. "I'm well aware. I wanted to give up, but now I know there's a new life, I can't do that." She finished mixing the batter and carefully poured four small circles onto the skillet.

"I think you and I should join forces," he finally said after a long period of silence. "Let's see how well we work together for a week or two and make some plans after that."

She nodded. "That would be nice." Truthfully, though, she knew she could be a teacher if all else failed.

His children had been playing down by the creek with the others in the group, and as they walked into the circle of wagons, they spotted Jane cooking over their campfire. The oldest, David, started running, with the other two following closely behind.

When David reached the fire, he stopped running. "Are you making food for us, Mrs. Davies?"

"I'm making Johnny cakes. I'm going to cook for your family at least until your pa can walk again." Jane grinned at the boy before carefully flipping each of the Johnny cakes.

David clapped, turning to his sisters who had arrived shortly after he did. "Mrs. Davies is going to cook for us while Pa is hurt! We need to hurt his other foot."

Jane laughed. "Now don't go hurting your pa. I will cook for you as long as you need me to."

"Forever," David said adamantly, folding his arms across his chest as if he was a young king and his word was law.

The two younger children—both girls—copied his stance, looking at her curiously. "I guess I'm cooking forever then." Jane grinned at the three. "Wash up. I'll have Johnny cakes ready in a few minutes, and you're going to want to eat them while theyre hot."

The three hurried off to wash their hands with big brother David helping the smaller children. "They're very well-mannered," Jane said.

Mr. Henderson nodded. "They're good children. Judy did a good job with them."

"I'm sure some of their manners came from you."

He shook his head. "I worked seven days a week back in Kentucky. There was no chance at all for me to teach them anything. They were usually asleep before I came in at the end of the day and were still sleeping when I left. That's why we wanted to start a business together. The children could help in small ways, but we'd always be together. Doesn't that sound lovely?"

Jane nodded. She understood having dreams washed away with a fickle turn of the river. That's how it had been for so many families on their journey. No more needed to be said as she fixed four plates, realizing there was no butter, so she ran back to her own wagon, and brought the treat.

The children were already eating the food with no honey or butter. "Let me finish fixing them, and they'll taste better."

David spoke with his mouth completely full, just after she'd complimented his manners. "'Sgood."

Mr. Henderson sighed. "Don't talk with your mouth full. You know better."

David nodded, waiting until he'd chewed the food in his mouth before making his apology. "I'm sorry!"

Mr. Henderson fell on his food as quickly as the children had. "This is delicious, Mrs. Davies. Thank you so much for making us a meal when you had just eaten."

Jane put some water on the fire to wash the dishes. "You were all hungry, I see. I'm going to my wagon to sleep under it for an hour, and then I'll start on supper. I have an idea for something that will taste good to all of us."

After lunch, the two little girls snuggled up together on the ground and slept. Mr. Henderson watched the children for a moment, before watching Mrs. Davies leave to return to her wagon. He was so thankful she had decided to help them. Perhaps she was right and having someone else to do for would help her stop thinking about the man she'd lost.

He hoped so anyway. He had an idea that he'd talk to her about as soon as he knew how well they worked together. On a journey such as this one, you could learn a great deal about someone very quickly.

He leaned back against the rock he was using to sit against, his mind going quickly. It would be harder for her because she'd just lost her husband, while Judy had died their first week out. If he'd had anything to go home to, he'd have gone home with his tail between his legs. Unfortunately, he'd sold all their belongings. They'd purchased the wagon and oxen, but he'd kept aside a good amount of money to help build his hotel. Perhaps he could make his wife's dream come true after all.

Chapter Two

Sunday, July 11th, 1852

God is watching over my family. I had just about given up on God and everything else, but a recent widow of our company brought me a pie today and proceeded to offer to cook for us. I could afford to pay Mrs. Prewitt to cook for us, but then I wouldn't have the money I need to build the hotel Judy fantasized about. I have to keep her dream since I couldn't keep her. I may even name the hotel after her, but I haven't decided that yet.

Mrs. Davies has said she'll cook for us as long as I need the help, and I'll still be able to drive, even with this ankle of mine, so the children will be fed well and looked after. I'm thankful for her offer as I had just decided to ask Mrs. Prewitt to make our meals, and I didn't want to dip into our hotel fund. Perhaps that would have been the right thing to do, but I like the idea of being able to see to my family.

I'm sure it's just pride speaking, but I can't shirk away from that any better than I can shed my skin and climb into another's.

The area where we are camped is beautiful. I've been told we'll stay over through tomorrow, so the men have time to hunt. The hunting and berry picking are better here than we've seen. It's truly a remarkable little place. I know I would like to settle my family here, but I'm not sure we'll make it all the way back here. It's been so hard on our family.

What most of the company doesn't know is that my Judy was expecting when she died. I lost two people with her death. Not just one. I miss my wife with everything inside me, and I pray that I will be able to move on without the debilitating grief soon. I know that is why I injured myself. My mind wasn't on what I was doing. I was thinking about Judy. But since I'm constantly in prayer, I know God will help me through this time. Just as he sent one of his angels to us in the form of Mrs. Davies.

After a short nap, from which Jane woke with a sense of purpose for the first time in a long while, she got up and took the ingredients needed to make the supper she had in mind at the Hendersons' camp. She collected rice, flour, seasoning, and the venison and walked over, stoking the fire that was still there.

Before doing anything else, she chopped the venison into tiny pieces that even the littlest of the Henderson family could eat. She knew three-year-old Alice from the daily walks, and she was certain the child wouldn't wait while anyone chopped up her food into manageable bites.

She hadn't fed the family much for their noon meal because she felt they should all eat a hearty meal tonight, and they would have meat, which would help all of them. Jane missed having meat with supper every night, but she was certain the children needed a change from the beans they so hated a great deal more than she did. They'd all have meat that night. And judging by the deer, elk, and bear hanging from the trees, they'd have dried meat for some time to come.

Jane went to the creek to collect water for their supper, and she coated the venison in flour before putting it into the pot she'd brought from her own supplies and browning it all, flipping it when necessary.

When the meat was almost finished, she put the rice on the fire in the big pot the other family had before she added water to the venison to make a thick gravy that would taste good over the rice.

She didn't realize Mr. Henderson was watching her until he spoke. "Why add water to the meat?" he asked.

"I'm making a gravy for the venison. It'll be far more appetizing over the rice that way." She frowned. "I should make a vegetable to go with it."

He shook his head. "The children won't eat them. They're going to be very happy with real food for a change."

"I'm happy to make something. There should be enough for the noon meal tomorrow as well. I always say if it's good once, it's good a second time."

He smiled. "Thank you for your kindness toward me and my children. I'd about given up on God because my prayers seemed to be ignored."

Jane took a deep breath. "Never give up on our Heavenly Father. He's the one who is giving us the strength to move a little further every day."

Mr. Henderson nodded at her but said nothing. She wasn't sure if he was agreeing with her or simply placating her, and at that moment, she didn't care. She'd said her piece.

Glancing under the wagon, she could tell that all three children were off playing again. All of the children were enjoying playing in the creek. It wasn't a hot day, but it was hot enough that the water would feel wonderful.

The venison and gravy were completely finished, and the rice was almost done when the children came back to camp. All three looked like they'd been in the creek with all their clothes on, but Jane didn't say a word. It wasn't her place.

David—the oldest—asked, "What are you making, Mrs. Davies? It sure does smell good!"

Jane smiled. "I'm making venison in a gravy to put over the rice. I think it will be delicious, though I've never cooked anything like it before. You'll have to tell me if it's good or not so I can decide if I'll ever make it again."

Alice pulled two fingers out of her mouth as she spoke for all of them. "No beans."

Jane laughed. "No beans tonight!"

Hattie, the middle child, shook her head. "No beans ever."

"I can't make that promise. We don't know how long our other food will stay good. I'll try not to make a lot of beans, though. Does that make you feel better?"

All three children nodded. When Jane started to fill plates for all of them, little Alice was practically dancing. She was so excited to get food that wasn't beans, and it was obvious to all of them.

For a moment, Jane considered taking her own food back to her camp to eat in solitude, but she knew it would be better for her to stay with the Hendersons. It was strange that she liked to be alone so much, even though she knew it was better for her to be with other people.

While they ate, Mr. Henderson talked to the children about what they'd done that day. "I picked some berries while the little kids were sleeping, and then we all played in the creek once they were awake," David said.

"I took a nap!" Alice said.

Hattie nodded. "I napped and played."

Jane was surprised at Mr. Henderson's next words. "What about you, Mrs. Davies? What did you do today?"

"I went to the church service, and then Mrs. Bedwell and I made several pies with the berries we picked yesterday. I brought your family a pie, fixed the noon meal, slept for a while, and came back here to fix supper. It was a normal non-traveling day."

"Has anyone said for certain if we're moving on tomorrow or spending another day hunting and gathering berries and firewood? It's nice to have some firewood again." It was better to burn firewood than buffalo chips, though they'd burned their share of the chips.

Jane shrugged. "I haven't talked to anyone since the noon meal, but I'll go ask around. Perhaps the children and I can pick some more berries this evening, and we can make another pie."

David smiled. "Can we have pie for dessert?"

Jane smiled. "If it's all right with your father, I'll slice it up."

All three children looked at their father. "Would that be all right, Pa?" David asked.

Mr. Henderson nodded. "You're all going to be spoiled by Mrs. Davies if she keeps making pies."

Seeing that the children had cleaned their plates and wanting to save as much of the meal as they could for the following day, Jane carefully removed the pie from the back of the wagon where she'd put it earlier and cut it into eight pieces. Then she carefully cut one of the pieces into two pieces, giving the girls the half pieces.

The children ate their pie greedily while Mr. Henderson savored every bite. "Let me know what you find out about when we move on," he said once he'd finished, and set his fork on the edge of his plate. "Thank you for our fine supper, Mrs. Davies. We're very appreciative."

"I was happy to do it," Jane responded. "As soon as I finish the dishes, I'll find out when we leave and decide if I can wait until tomorrow to pick berries or if I should go ahead and do it tonight."

Mr. Henderson nodded, reaching for the crutches Dr. Bentley had given him to use. Thankfully, he was the only one who needed them at the moment. Jane watched him struggle but didn't offer to help. A man had his pride, after all.

After finishing the dishes, Jane walked toward the Bedwells' camp to ask about whether they would leave in the morning or wait a day. She spotted Katie and smiled. It was nice to have a true friend on a journey like this. "Katie!" she called out as she approached the camp.

Katie smiled, waving to her. "I saw you cooking for the Hendersons. I think it's good you have someone to care for."

Jane nodded. "I believe it is. Tell me, did the captains decide to leave in the morning, or wait until Tuesday."

"The decision was made to move in the morning, but we'll stop an hour early so we can hunt and get more berries. This part of the country is much cooler, so we can start early, take a long noon break and continue our walk in the early evening when it's cooler again. During our break, we can hunt and collect fruit that we see. George said the next stop is only about thirty miles away, and we'll take two days to do it. That way we can stop and replenish supplies along the way. There's some sort of strange springs there from what he's said. There'll be a camping point halfway for people who want to stop along the way like we are."

"That'll be nice. All right. I promised Mr. Henderson I'd let him know as soon as I found out, but he's not quite back to camp yet. Would you like me to wipe the dishes while I wait for him to return?"

Katie shook her head. "No need. I can handle them. You're going to want to get as many berries as you can before we leave in the morning. There's another patch past where we were picking them last night. That will be the best place to go, I think. Just make sure you leave some for the other companies."

"I will. I wish we had time to dry the berries before moving on." Jane started back to the Hendersons' camp as she saw Mr. Henderson drop the crutches and sit down beside the rock he'd been using to lean against. "Thanks for the information, and I'll talk to you later!" she called over her shoulder as she headed away.

Mr. Henderson was fussing with the bandage on his ankle. "Do you need some help with that?" Jane asked. "I could try to do it or run and fetch the doctor for you."

"No, thank you. I need to learn to see to it myself." When he removed the bandage, she could see swelling and bruising on all sides of the ankle, and her heart immediately went out to him.

"That's a really bad sprain!" she said. "I could bring some of the cold water from the creek to soak it in."

He shook his head. "I don't think I need that. Doc gave me a little laudanum if I need it, but so far, I've managed to avoid it."

Jane shuddered. "My father took that when he broke his back. He acted like a crazy man for three weeks before he finally started healing. I don't think you should take it." She'd rather he used whiskey for the pain, and she was no believer in alcohol for anything.

Mr. Henderson nodded. "I don't plan to. But I have it if I need it."

"Is there any other way I can help tonight? I want to get some berries picked before it's dark."

"There's a basket in the very back of my wagon. Take my children and race them. That's how Judy got them to do their chores quickly, and it always worked."

"I will do that. Are they down by the creek?"

He chuckled. "By it or in it. I don't think they really know the difference right now."

"None of the children do. I'll get them to help. I'll use my schoolmarm voice if I have to."

"Good! Collect lots so we can have more pies."

Jane was smiling as she headed toward her wagon, surprised she still remembered how. Her grieving had completely taken her over for so long, that it was hard for her to believe there was an entire spectrum of emotions she'd forgotten.

She got her berry basket from the back and went in search of the Henderson children. Following the sounds of laughter down to the creek, she stood at the edge, shielding her eyes from the sun. There were at least twenty children in the creek, most of whom she knew by name. She watched them frolic for a moment before calling out,

"David, Hattie, and Alice? I need you to come out and pick berries with me."

Though the children looked saddened, they immediately got out of the water, dripping their way toward her. David took the basket from her, and she realized then the children hadn't even removed their shoes. "You can't wear shoes in the creek!"

David shrugged. "The water's cold, and we didn't want our toes to get cold."

Jane hid the laugh that threatened to come out. "You'll ruin your shoes that way. Come on. I know where a good patch is, and we can make another pie if we get enough berries."

The children looked excited as soon as she said the word that motivated them beyond all others: pie. The four of them went and collected berries as quickly as they could. "Remember to only get the ripe ones. We want there to be more berries for the next company who comes through here."

David nodded. "I'll make sure the girls do it right. We won't pick the berries that should be left behind for others."

Watching the boy with his little sisters, Jane felt her heart ache for him. He'd had to grow up much too quickly due to his mother's death. The children still had sad looks on their faces most of the time, but there they were, picking berries as if their next meal depended on it.

Sometimes she wondered if this "death march" as Mrs. Mitchell called it was worth the free land. She knew Adam had considered it the most important journey in the world. Had he been right? Maybe someday she'd know the answer to that, but it wouldn't be until they'd settled in on that new land. She just hoped it would be soon.

Chapter Three

Monday, July 12th, 1852

We are leaving the spot the company has chosen to settle in this morning. I'm not sure how I feel about that. I so wish I could just stay here and allow someone else to stake my claim for me, but it just doesn't work that way. I need to go along and sign the paperwork myself.

This valley is so peaceful. I feel like I'm leaving a piece of myself behind as we keep traveling, knowing there's a great deal of walking left to do before we can come back to Clover Creek. I do hope no one will stake a claim here before us, but I suppose a larger settlement wouldn't hurt anyone.

I have been helping the Henderson family. In a few minutes the whistle will blow, and it will be time for everyone to wake and start cooking breakfasts and hitching up wagons. Mr. Henderson told me that he had someone who would hitch the wagon for him, but he does need my help with breakfast.

It's amazing how children so small can be so thankful that they are getting a good meal that isn't beans. I myself have been tired of beans for a long while, but I can't complain. I'm still alive, and I have a babe growing within me.

I was just told we are starting later than usual today so the meat from yesterday can be seen to. Even though I don't hunt, and I don't have a man to hunt for me, no one minds sharing their meat with me. And no one will mind sharing with the Hendersons until Mr. Henderson is back on his feet and hunting with the rest of the men. His ankle looks terrible. I don't think I've ever seen so much bruising in my life. I do worry it might be broken, but the doc said it wasn't. I'm not sure how he knows without being able to see into the foot, but he seems convinced. I will bow to his greater knowledge on the subject.

I would write more, but I must start breakfast and join the other women in drying the meat that was hunted while we were here. We must not waste even a morsel if we want to make it all the way to Oregon City and back this year.

Jane felt rushed to make breakfast and help with the meat drying process. She wasn't sure why they weren't just staying for another day, but she trusted the captains to do what was best for the entire company, and not just what was best for her. She mixed up Johnny cakes at her camp, and then carried the batter over as soon as the whistle blew to let them all know it was time to wake. It wasn't even dawn yet, but that was a good time to wake up when you were walking twenty miles per day.

She found the Hendersons' frying pan, stoked the fire that was still burning slightly in the circle of rocks, and then she put a pat of butter into the middle of the pan before setting it on the stove.

She would have to make more butter that day, but the best way to do it was to just put the fresh cream in a bucket and tie it to the bottom of the wagon. It would be butter before they reached the place where they'd rest for the day.

Jane hoped that most of the berry picking could be done as they walked along. It would be nice not to waste time as they walked. You didn't have to walk fast when you were following oxen, just faster than the critters did.

She looked down and spotted one of the Scotts' kittens playing in her skirts. It was hard to hold back a laugh, but she somehow managed. No one needed laughing quite that early in the morning.

She'd never been an early morning person, but this journey had taught her to be. She wanted to write in her journal each morning before breakfast, and she made certain she'd kept that little promise to herself. Every morning she'd written. There were tears that stained many pages after her dear Adam had died, but she had written no matter what.

Jane was aware of the camp moving around her, with people hurrying off to relieve themselves in tall grass or behind some trees. She jumped when she was directly spoken to, and then she laughed at herself.

"What's for breakfast this morning, Mrs. Davies?" Looking up, Jane saw Mr. Henderson watching her.

"I'm just doing Johnny cakes again," she answered. "We're leaving a little later than planned so we can dry out some of the meat that the men hunted here, which means the berries can also dry some. I thought it best to do a quick breakfast and join the other women to help dry the meat."

"I think that sounds wise. It was lovely to wake up to someone fixing our breakfast this morning. If I haven't said it before, I'll say it now. Thank you for being so generous with your time and helping my family as we journey along."

"It gives me a reason to wake in the mornings," she said softly, certain he'd understand.

"It was that way for me right after I lost my Judy. It's a hard thing to get beyond when you're walking like this...surrounded by well-meaning people who want to make everything better for you." He rubbed the last of his neck. "Looks like my other crutch is too far out of reach. I don't suppose you'd be willing to help me out?"

"Oh, of course. When will you be allowed to put weight on that foot?"

"Doc said after we get to the soda water springs that are coming up. I'm not quite sure when that is."

"We plan to be there tomorrow night, according to what I've been told. It's a thirty-mile journey from here, and we'll do just fifteen miles for the next two days to reach there on Tuesday night." Jane carefully flipped the Johnny cakes onto five plates and fixed her own cake just how she liked it.

Mr. Henderson and his children each took a plate and fixed their own cakes. "Will we have time to play in the creek before we start out today?" David asked politely.

"We will, but it's cold right now. It would probably be best if you didn't. The women are going to quickly start some meat drying before we go." Jane wondered if they would find a way for the meat to keep drying as they walked. There was no way the meat would be all the way dry before they left that morning.

Mr. Henderson frowned. "I think to make that work, we'll have to hang a string on the back of each wagon, with several pieces of meat hanging from it."

Jane frowned. "I don't understand. Wouldn't the string just dangle and get dirty?"

"Oh, I meant to hang one end of the string to one side of the wagon, and the other end to the other side of the wagon. Does that make sense?"

"Absolutely. If no one has come up with something else, I'll suggest that. We certainly want to have as much meat dried or drying as we can."

After cleaning the dishes, Jane joined the other women who had gathered between Margaret Prewitt's camp and that of the Scotts.

"How are we going to do this?" she asked hesitantly. Her voice had disappeared for a while after her Adam had passed, but now she felt that she could speak for herself again. Finally.

Several ideas were thrown out, but none of them seemed plausible to Jane. Jane told the others what Mr. Henderson had suggested, and they all agreed that was the best idea.

The wagons rolled out two hours later than usual, but there was still a distinct chill in the air. To no one's surprise the children hadn't played in the creek for long. The air was just too frigid for that.

They didn't stop for the noon meal, so Jane took a cup of cold coffee, and cold food from the night before up to Mr. Henderson. "That's going to have to hold you until we stop for our evening meal."

Mr. Henderson nodded. "I think it will do just fine. You have my thanks, Mrs. Davies."

"Should I have the girls sit on the back of the wagon to eat and get their naps?"

"I would appreciate that."

Once the girls were settled on the back of the wagon with their bowls of food, she tracked down David and handed his to him. "It's cold but should still taste good."

"Thank you, Mrs. Davies."

Taking the rest of the food for herself, Jane walked as she ate. The other women were all doing the same. Mary fell into step beside Jane, chatting with her. "I'm glad you're taking on the Hendersons," Mary said. "We were talking after church Sunday about who could feed them until Mr. Henderson could walk again, and when I looked up, you were there helping out. Thank you."

"It helped me a lot when Mrs. Bedwell took me under her wing and fed me after Adam's death. There were a few days I wasn't sure how I was going to be able to keep going."

Mary nodded. "That's happening more than it should in our little camp. I wish I had words of wisdom, but what can you say to make someone feel better after something so awful?"

Jane nodded, taking another bite of her meal. "I was going to be a rancher's wife once we reached Oregon. Now I'll have to go back to being a schoolmarm, and someone else will have to see to my baby all day. It doesn't seem right."

"No, it doesn't. What can I do to help you?" Mary asked.

"Nothing. Doing for others makes me feel better than anything anyone could do for me. I had no idea it would make me feel as good as it has."

Mary smiled, nodding. "That's how I am as well. If I can do something for someone else, I can keep going. If I'm completely on my own, there's no way I can."

Jane sighed. "Why are women made this way?"

"No idea! Remember if you need something, or even just need a little help with the Hendersons, I'm here, and I'll help in any way I can."

"I think that's my favorite part about walking the trail. We have made connections with each other, and when we all settle together, it will just feel like we're continuing this journey...with friends and family."

"I'm your sister," Mary said with a wink. "Now I need to run back and see if my ma needs help with any of the little ones. I promised when I married Bob that I would be certain to help out just as much as I did before the wedding. We take supper with my family every night, and I help with the cooking. It's better that way."

Jane nodded, as Mary slowed down so her mother could catch up with her. As Jane walked, she realized that for the first time, she really did feel as if she was part of a big family on the trail. Everyone looked out for her, and now she was looking out for others. Life seemed to come full circle often, and this circle was a good one.

David caught up with Jane then and gave her his empty bowl. "It was delicious, Mrs. Davies. Do you want me to put my dishes and yours in the back of the wagon by the girls?"

"That would be wonderful. Are you going to nap today?"

David scoffed. "I'm seven! Naps are for babies."

"Oh, I'm sorry, I didn't realize. Of course, you won't nap." She hid a grin as the boy hurried ahead and found their wagon and put the dishes into it.

She held back for a moment, and fell into step with Mrs. Cauldron, a lovely woman with twin boys who were absolute menaces.

"How are you doing today, Mrs. Cauldron?"

"Oh, doing well. I had to fish the boys out of the creek this morning, but other than that, everything is good. I'm sure the boys will end up being well-behaved, won't they?"

Jane couldn't hold back a laugh. "As a schoolmarm, I've noticed that the boys who cause the most trouble when they're little, tend to be the hardest workers later in life. They just have too much energy, and they put it into mischief when they're little, but as they grow, they find much better uses for all that energy. Why, I wouldn't be surprised if one of your boys became a minister."

Mrs. Cauldron laughed, shaking her head. "That's not going to happen. How could it? They can't sit still long enough to memorize one scripture, let alone learning all they needed to know to preach God's word."

"You may be surprised," Jane said softly. She loved that Mrs. Cauldron didn't have romantic notions about her boys. She didn't expect them to act perfectly. She knew who they were.

"Have you seen my sister this afternoon?" Mrs. Cauldron asked. "I hope she's not sitting in the back of her wagon reading again. She needs to get to know people."

"I saw her riding with the doc earlier. They seemed to be having an in-depth discussion about something."

"Of course. The doc is training Betty to be a nurse for him. She loves learning, so she rides with him, and he teaches her often. And she's reading all his medical books."

"Sounds like she's going to be doing a lot of good. I'm glad she's not afraid to learn all that stuff. I think I would be."

Mrs. Cauldron shook her head. "Not Betty. If there's something to be learned, she's the first to say she wants to learn it. I always thought she'd be a good doctor, but who would go see a woman doctor? The notion is ridiculous. But Betty could do it if she put her mind to it."

Jane smiled. "It's nice to know we have a woman of her intelligence along. I wouldn't mind learning from her."

"We just have to convince her she can teach others, even though she's shy."

Chapter Four

Monday, July 12th, 1852

We left Clover Creek this morning and headed toward the carbonated water springs that are promised thirty miles up the trail. Thank heavens for Mrs. Davies, who made us breakfast, and then fed us all the noon meal while we continued on. When we reached the fifteen miles the captains scheduled for today, we were atop a summit of some sort, and we made our camp here.

The hills were steep, but they were nothing compared to Big Hill where I hurt my ankle. Instead, they were a steady incline, but not so sharp. We'll go down the other side tomorrow, and I'm not certain how ready I am to go down a steep hill again. Thankfully, I won't need to worry about the children, because along with cooking for us, Mrs. Davies seems to have taken over the supervision of the children as well.

For supper, we had some of the meat that was hunted at Clover Creek, along with potatoes and a rich gravy. I find Mrs. Davies is a wonderful cook, perhaps only true because I spent so long trying to eat my own cooking and listening to my children complain about everything I made.

We'll reach Soda Springs Complex tomorrow where there will be more food for us to purchase. I don't mind buying food now that there is someone who can cook it properly and not burn it the way I do. I do think I need to suggest a more permanent arrangement to Mrs. Davies, but I'll wait the week out like I initially thought. You can learn a great deal about someone in the span of a week.

After supper that evening, all the men who were able set out with their rifles, hoping to get more bears, elk, deer, and buffalo. On the old map Adam had, all were indicated to be good hunting there. Hopefully, they'd have enough dried meat to last them all the way to Oregon City and back by the time they left the area.

Jane sat with Mr. Henderson and his children as the men went out to hunt. She saw women disappear with their berry baskets, so she suggested she take the children. "Would it be all right if I took the children berry picking?" she asked softly. "I think it helps the little ones to appreciate their meals when they take part in harvesting them."

Mr. Henderson nodded. "That would be very nice, if you don't mind. I'm sure you can pick more on your own."

"I could. But then the children wouldn't learn."

He waved his hand as if dismissing her. Jane took the basket from the back of the Henderson's wagon and hurried to her own for her basket, and then she went in search of the children, who were busy collecting kindling and small branches for their fires as they moved along.

"Put your wood near the campfire, but not so close it could catch fire, and then come berry picking with me. The more berries we collect, the more pies we'll have on our journey."

All three children ran back to camp and came to her. "David, carry the basket. Alice and Hattie, pick as many ripe berries as you can. We'll have a race to see if I can do more than you three."

David let out an excited whoop. "We're going to win!"

Jane just laughed, pleased that the children were ready to try to beat her. They'd get more berries that way. She led the children out past the other women, and the four of them picked huckleberries. The berries were tiny and it would take a great deal to make a pie, but Jane didn't mind. The children were learning the importance of working to help the family, and she was proud of them.

When both baskets were mostly full, Jane declared a tie, and they hurried back to camp to show off their berries. Katie met Jane when she was almost back to the Hendersons' camp. "What berries did you find? I found a grove of raspberries. Some were ripe, but most weren't. I'd happily trade half of my raspberries for some huckleberries."

Jane smiled, nodding emphatically. "That sounds wonderful." The children hurried on back to camp, while Jane and Katie exchanged berries so they'd each have some of both varieties.

When Jane returned to the Hendersons' camp, Mr. Henderson was on his feet without his crutches. He wobbled a bit, and Jane hurried to his side to keep him from falling. "Are you supposed to be on that foot yet?" she asked, giving him her stern schoolteacher look.

He shrugged. "Doc said it would be fine if it didn't hurt me."

"And is it hurting you?"

"More than I care to admit." He sighed. "I think I'm going to be using crutches for a few days yet."

"I don't think that's a problem. You're driving every day, and I can help with the children."

"I know. I just feel like I'm not doing my part, and that's part of what we all agreed to before we left Independence."

"Yes, it is," Jane said. "But everyone has been sick or injured along the way, or even lost family members. We're moving as a group to help one another. You're not slowing anyone down, so I would think all is good."

"That's probably true. I have to ask that you take some of the money I have saved for the hotel and go get some fresh food tomorrow when we get to Soda Springs Complex. Would you mind?"

"I'd be happy to. Do you know what you want me to get? Or should I use my own judgment."

Mr. Henderson pursed his lips. "Use your judgment. I'll give you ten dollars, and you buy as much as you can. I think I'm low on coffee."

"I have coffee. I'll look and see if it's worth spending money on more."

He frowned. "You don't mind sharing?"

She shook her head. "Not at all. I'm more of a tea drinker than a coffee drinker. The coffee was for Adam. Which do you have your children drink?"

"My wife had them on tea only, but since I've taken over, they've been drinking coffee. I can't be bothered to make both."

"I'll switch them back to tea. I think that's easier for small children to drink." Jane still couldn't drink coffee easily. To her it was a bitter grown-up drink for people other than herself. Tea was her favorite. "I've swapped some of the huckleberries we picked this evening for raspberries. I hope you like raspberries because I think I'm making raspberry pancakes in the morning."

He grinned. "That sounds so much better than Johnny cakes. I shouldn't complain because they are filling and keep me going, but they're not my favorite breakfast."

"I'll try to keep that in mind. I wish I'd been smart enough to bring some chickens along so I could have fresh eggs along the way."

"They're so hard to keep corralled though. I wouldn't have chickens along for anything."

"I can see the logic in that." She still wished she had chickens though. It would be nice to start a henhouse with fresh eggs every morning, and pullets for their meals.

"Will you serve what we had left from supper for the noon meal again tomorrow?"

She nodded. "It seems the easiest way to do things. We have only fifteen miles to go tomorrow, but this hill looks awfully steep."

"It is. That's all right though. We'll make it down the hill and to the next town. I'm excited to see the springs so many have talked about. I think the children will enjoy them."

"Is it just one spring or are there multiple springs?" she asked, not having done the kind of research Mr. Henderson or her late husband had done on the trail.

"There are many. Indian lore says they have healing properties. Now, I don't know if that's true, but I'm willing to try anything. Maybe if I soak my foot in one of the springs, I'll be able to walk more easily."

"That's sounds interesting. Do you know if the springs are hot or cold?"

"That information has not drifted my way. I do know there are hot springs along the way, but I have no idea where they'll be."

"I suppose it will be fun to find out in the morning." Jane hid a yawn behind her hand. "I'm going to use a bit of drinking water to wash our berries, and then I'm going to head to my wagon for sleep. I can't get used to sleeping out in the open like so many do. I want to be under my wagon where I feel safe."

"I can understand that. Before I hurt myself, I put up a tent for the children every night, but now the girls sleep inside the wagon, and David and I sleep under it. He likes it a lot. Feels like he's a man sleeping under the wagon."

She smiled. "I can understand that perfectly." Getting to her feet, she picked up the two baskets, and took a small amount of their drinking water. After washing the berries, she put them into the back of the wagon, and headed to her own makeshift home. There was no point in changing clothes, as she would wear the same dress the following day. Instead, she pulled out her blanket and curled up under the wagon. She would have liked to sleep under the stars, but it didn't feel safe with Indians and bears running around.

She was up early the following morning as was her practice. She would have liked to sleep until well past noon, but the opportunity hadn't presented itself in a good long while.

She found the fixings for pancakes in the back of her wagon, as well as coffee, and she headed over to the Hendersons' camp where she started breakfast. By the time the whistle sounded to wake them all, Jane had the fire going, and the smell of bacon permeated the air.

David woke up, and the first thing he said was, "Bacon. Pa, she's making bacon!"

Jane grinned to herself at the enthusiasm in the boy's voice. It was hard not to have all the comforts of home, but there was a bit of bacon that didn't have to have the mold trimmed from it. Hopefully, bacon would be one of those foods she could buy in Soda Springs Complex.

After a quick breakfast and an even quicker cleanup, they were on their way, well before the time they usually started. The captains had decided not to spend more than a night in the town coming up, so everyone would need to get supplies when they arrived that evening, which meant starting early and moving quickly down the road.

Not that they could really move quickly. The oxen had one speed: slow. They would just take no noon break again. Thankfully she'd made enough to last the family until they reached the little town ahead.

The company had passed up many of the forts and towns along the way, hoping to be able to make good enough time to be settled in before winter. This time, there were too many people out of food, and they had no choice. But still, they'd only take a few hours to replenish their supplies before they moved on toward Oregon City.

The day's pace was difficult, at least at first as they had to descend the hill, and each person was careful where each step landed. It would be an easier trek if there weren't so many mountains between Independence and Oregon City, she thought for the fiftieth time that week. It seemed like the mountains had crept up on them, and they were forced to learn to climb and descend hills whether they were ready for them or not.

No one was hurt during the descension, which Jane felt was a minor miracle in and of itself. And then they headed up and down and around many more hills before they reached their destination.

After setting up camp for the evening, Jane went to Mr. Henderson to see what he would have her do. He gave her ten dollars in coins, and she went to find food to sustain her and his little family for the next two and a half months. It felt like her journey should be over because she'd found her future home, but the journey to Oregon City and back wasn't something they could ignore or skip if they wanted to legally own their land in Clover Creek.

Jane went off to trade with the traders and the few Indians that were camped there, waiting for emigrants such as themselves.

She was able to purchase a great deal of potatoes, flour, and more bacon. She was thankful the old bacon could be thrown away. After taking the goods back to camp, and wishing she'd brought a young man to carry her purchases for her, she fixed their supper, thankful to have been one of the first of the women shopping there.

"Do you need more ammunition?" she asked Mr. Henderson.

He shook his head. "I bought three times what we were told to buy. I assume you still have some of Adam's ammunition?"

Jane nodded. "I've never personally traded with an Indian before, but they were the ones to sell me the bacon and potatoes. Should I get more corn meal?" Suddenly she was second guessing herself, wondering what the best things she could have purchased were. "I still have more than two dollars."

"I think more cornmeal would be good. I prefer wheat flour, but the corn meal lasts longer, and we should be able to eat all the way to Oregon City on it. We can get more provisions there, of course."

"Oh, good. I'll run and fetch some cornmeal." This time, she went to Katie and asked for her son's Stanley's help to bring her purchases back to camp. He was more than willing to help, and that pleased her.

The huge sack of cornmeal was just what they needed, and she instructed Stanley to put it into the back of her wagon, and not that of the Hendersons. It would be better that way because she wasn't taking up space that his girls would sleep in.

Stanley offered to empty their drinking water and add new to their barrels, and she was very thankful, but the captains had warned them that drinking too much of the carbonated water would make them sick. They couldn't let the oxen have much of it either.

Then she took the hands of each of the Henderson girls, and they went and looked at the spring. It looked like someone had carbonated the water artificially and then pumped it into the ground. She couldn't wait to write in her journal about the marvel she'd seen there on the edge of the trail. It was truly a sight to see!

Chapter Five

Tuesday, July 13th, 1852

We are camped in the most wondrous place I have ever been! There are many springs full of carbonated water here, including one called beer springs. They truly seem as if someone has artificially carbonated water and poured it into the ground to be used by all. Most of the springs are cold, but one spring is hot, and many of the women are doing their laundry there, even though it was done on Sunday. I am not quite so ambitious.

We were able to buy some supplies here, and the Hendersons' and I will be set until we reach Oregon City. I must say, I will be very thankful when we finally reach and see that elephant!

The Henderson children and I are becoming more comfortable with one another every day, and Mr. Henderson seems to enjoy my company as well as my cooking. Is it shameful to say I would like for him to ask me to marry him so I no longer have to worry so much about what will become of my child and me at the end of our journey? I do know we'll settle in Clover Creek, but will I have to teach school again? I know I can't homestead on my own. Not with an infant. But if I were to marry Mr. Henderson, whose first name I do not yet know, that worry would be taken off my shoulders.

I would only agree to a marriage in name only. I could not have relations with a man other than my Adam. I believe I will die still loving him. I know it may seem impractical to many, but perhaps it will work. When you have a love as strong as mine with Adam, it changes your life and spoils you for other men. I am spoiled.

Tomorrow we will head further along the Bear River, which has been our compass since we left Clover Creek. I pray that there will be another body of water to travel along, as the water makes the journey easier and less deadly. I should look at the map my Adam kept in his Bible. I will do that before I cook the morning meal. And then I will know if we will still travel along a river or if we will be on dry land the entire time.

After closing her journal, Jane stuck her head into the back of her wagon to find her late husband's Bible with the map he'd tucked neatly inside. According to the map, they had another short period of following the Bear River, and then they would travel along the Portneuf River for a short while. After that, they would be on the banks of a large lake that didn't seem to be labeled on her map. She would find out when she arrived what the lake was called. Everyone would know before they arrived. That's how it was in their company.

She was true to her word and made pancakes with raspberries for breakfast that morning. The children gobbled them up quickly, and Jane made a few more. They should be able to eat their fill in the morning when they were going to walk twenty miles or so. It was only right.

Everyone had said the day would be an arduous one, with a huge summit they had to walk over, but they would end the day near some healing hot springs, and she loved the idea of taking a hot bath for free.

She joined with Katie and Hannah for the day's trek, not at all surprised when the captains announced another day without a noon break. The days without a break were much harder for everyone involved, but it would make it so they had more time that evening with the hot springs available.

The captain had said that the men would bathe while the women made their suppers, and then the women could bathe. It seemed strange to Jane, thinking about bathing with so many other women, but she wasn't going to complain. A hot bath! Who could ask for more?

Jane made a supper of bacon, gravy, and biscuits. She knew it wasn't the healthiest thing to feed the family, but sometimes you made what you had, and she had plenty of flour and bacon. They could eat this meal every day for a week, and she would still feel like they had enough to make many more meals. She knew the children would enjoy the diversity of food other than beans. It would be impossible to avoid cooking the staple for the rest of their journey, but she would do her best not to overdo it.

Mr. Henderson wasn't able to go down to the hot spring with the other men, as his ankle was still bothering him. Jane grinned when Pastor Scott and Mr. Prewitt approached the camp, and made a chair with their hands, hauling Mr. Henderson off to the hot springs, with his loud protests ringing in her ears.

After he returned, they had supper, and then she and the girls went down to the hot springs. Hattie and Alice each dipped a toe into the water, but they declared it too hot to bathe in.

Jane had no qualms. She stripped down to her drawers and climbed into the hot pool along with the other women, who had all chosen to preserve their modesty in the same way.

Mrs. Mitchell pulled out a bar of soap and washed her hair, then passed the bar around the hot pot. It was wonderful. All the women laughed and joked as they sank into the water, completely submerging themselves to get the suds from their hair.

Jane smiled. "This journey wouldn't be half so difficult if we could sink into one of these every night."

Everyone agreed. Eventually, they each climbed from the hot pot and let themselves drip dry in the waning sunlight. "I cannot think of a better way to end our day," Hannah said happily. "It felt as if the babe was spinning around inside me. I think she liked the water too."

"She?" Mary asked. "Are you wishing a girl as a first child on the good pastor?"

Hannah nodded. "I am. I'm not even ashamed of it."

Laughter was heard all around the pool as the women donned their dresses over wet drawers to head back to the men. "I wish we'd have time to do this again in the morning," Margaret said longingly.

"I'm always up before the whistle blows. I'm certain I'll be here before we leave," Jane said.

Several of the women agreed to meet there the following morning. "We do have to feed our children, though," Margaret said.

"We do! But I think we can bathe and then feed the children and the men. I suppose we should feed the men," Mrs. Mitchell said to everyone's amusement.

"I cannot think of a lovelier way to finish the day or start the next. I wish I could settle where there was a hot pool right next to my house, and I could go out and enjoy the waters whenever I felt like it," Penelope said. "I would be the happiest woman alive."

They all laughed as they headed back to camp. Jane was glad she'd taken the time to wash the supper dishes before she'd gone off to play in the water. It was best that everyone startled settling down for the night.

Jane helped the little girls into the back of their wagon, and made sure David was settled underneath before heading back to her own wagon. She did like helping the other family, but sometimes she was ready to be alone in her own camp at nighttime, and this was one of those times.

She settled under her wagon, thinking about the wonderful day she'd just had, ending in such a perfect way. She felt energized to take on more of the trail, though she knew there were still months of travel ahead of her. Her legs didn't ache quite as much from all the walking as they had done before. Perhaps the springs were healing after all!

She couldn't help but think about how much Adam would have loved the hot pots and this part of the journey. If only she hadn't lost him. Life would never be the same for her now that he was gone.

Across camp, Matthew Henderson was thinking about what a good woman Mrs. Davies was, and how good she'd been with his children. He couldn't keep waiting to ask her to be his bride. Some other man would notice how helpful she was and want her for his own wife.

He decided then and there to talk to her the next day about it. It seemed quick, but he knew better than letting the grass grow under his feet. And his ankle was so much better after the hot springs, he could even walk with her a bit away from the camp to have their talk.

The doc had said not to count on his ankle staying better, but he knew it was healed. God had given him two miracles that week. A healed ankle and Mrs. Davies. She had already made his life better.

As usual, Jane woke early the following morning, and after a brief note in her journal, she rushed to the hot pots to see only Margaret Prewitt and Hannah Scott there. "Where's everyone else?" Jane asked, as she stripped down to her drawers.

Hannah grinned. "Sleeping! It's hard to believe I once favored being awake late into the night."

Margaret shook her head at her friend. "Funny that she's learning to be a good little pastor's wife, isn't it?"

Jane grinned. "I think she had it in her all the while!"

Hannah laughed. "No, I didn't. I learned to fake it for Jed."

After their frolic in the hot pot, they all returned to their own camps, and Jane gathered the ingredients she'd need for breakfast. She was surprised to hear the whistle blow when she was on her way to the Hendersons' camp. Did she really spend a full hour in the hot pot?

She quickly made pancakes, having vowed she would make them every morning for a while, as Mr. Henderson preferred them to Johnny cakes.

As soon as they were all fed and the breakfast dishes were washed, Mr. Henderson surprised Jane. "Would you take a walk with me?"

Jane nodded. "You can walk now?"

"The hot pot did wonders for my ankle. Doc says it won't last long, but I refuse to believe him."

Jane noted that he was still limping as they walked away from the pots to the other side of the trail. "Have I done something to displease you?" she asked.

"No, not at all. To the contrary, I wanted to ask you an important question. I know this is going to seem to be coming suddenly, but I'd like to ask you to be my wife—in name only, of course. I don't think either of us are ready to give up on our lost loves. I like how you are with my children, and I know you'd do better with a man to protect you...and we do like to eat in my family..." He felt as if he was making a mess of things, but he wasn't sure how one should propose to someone he barely knew.

Jane had hoped this would happen. It really would be best for both of them. "I will under one condition."

"What's that?" he asked, frowning at her.

"You have to tell me what your first name is. I'm not one of those women who would refer to the man she was married to by his last name...whether the marriage was in name only or not."

He laughed softly. "It's Matthew. I can't believe you've helped me this much and you don't know my Christian name."

"I'm Jane, Matthew. And yes, I'll marry you, but it will have to be in name only. It hasn't been that long since I lost my Adam."

"I understand. More than anything I want someone I can expect to cook for my family and raise my children."

"You'll have that in me. You don't mind that I'm expecting?"

"Not even a little bit. It means you were happy in your marriage. I would like to reconsider things after your babe is born. Perhaps then we can make the marriage a real one."

Jane nodded. "We can talk about that when the time comes."

"Would you like to marry this evening, after we have our supper?"

"That would be acceptable. Should I keep my wagon? Or should we combine everything to make it easier on both of us?"

"I believe we should combine. But that can wait until our day off, if you'd like."

She shook her head. "No, it's only Thursday. There's no need for my wagon to be driven for two more days."

"Tonight then. The other women will help?"

"Yes, of course. I've helped them when they needed it. I feel like we're all a big family, and the other women are the sisters of my heart."

He walked back toward camp with her keeping the pace beside him. "You're limping much more heavily than you were."

He sighed. "I know. I should have listened to the doc. I do feel as if I can go on without the crutches, though."

"That's a good thing. Shall we tell the children?"

"Yes, of course." Matthew hadn't thought of what it would be like to tell his youngsters that he was marrying again. He was sure they'd be happy because they'd have a permanent cook, but they sometimes surprised him.

They told the children as soon as they got back to camp. David was the only one with something to say about it. "Good. We need someone who can cook."

Jane laughed. "I'm glad to know my role within your family," she said, grinning at Matthew.

"Help me hitch up the oxen, David," Matthew said as he limped toward where the oxen were corralled.

"Yes, Pa. You walk better than you did, but you still don't walk very good."

"Very well, and you're right. The hot pot did a great job, but I don't think it was a job that will last long. I'll have to wait until it heals properly before I do anything too much."

Jane was with the little girls, and Hattie looked at her shyly. "Will you read stories to me before bed like my mama used to?"

"Of course, I will. I love to read. Do you know how?"

Hattie shook her head while little Alice stood with two fingers in her mouth, watching the other two. "I want to learn soon."

"I used to be a schoolteacher. How about we start learning to read?"

"I'd like that!"

Alice obviously wasn't interested in learning to read, but she went to Jane and leaned against her, the first two fingers of her right hand in her mouth as usual. Jane knew Alice would be the one to rely on her the most.

Chapter Six

Thursday, June 15th, 1852

I asked Jane Davies to marry me this morning, and she agreed, so we had a quiet little ceremony tonight. My ankle is doing some better after the hot springs last night, but not as much better as I would have hoped by this point. I am thankful for the help Jane has given my family, and I am returning the favor by giving her my name and protection. The protection won't start until I'm better healed of course.

She is off with the children now, consolidating her supplies and belongings into our wagon, and hers will stay alongside the trail. We've spotted so many wagons along the way, and I always wonder why they were abandoned. Did the entire family die? Did one of the adults die leaving the other free to marry another? There's no way of knowing, but it gives me something to think about as I drive the oxen.

Today was a normal day for us. We travelled along the Portneuf River and made over half of the thirty-nine miles that must be walked between today and tomorrow. We'll be on this river for some time, but we're all thankful for the water it gives us.

I sometimes wish Jane didn't have to walk along the trail and could ride somewhere, given her condition, but there is no other way. And I let Judy walk knowing of her condition without giving it a second thought. I'm not certain why I think of Jane as frailer than my darling Judy, but it seems as if it's the case. I will make sure she has some rest time once we get back to Clover Creek, and I pray that will happen sooner than everyone expects.

Jane moved the last of her belongings from the wagon she and Adam had purchased into the Hendersons' wagon. It felt strange to let the wagon go, but they would take the oxen she and Adam had purchased with them. She salvaged all the coffee that was left, and she knew they'd have enough to reach Oregon City where they could get a few more supplies.

The bad thing about getting supplies along the trail was how dearly they had to pay. Everything was much less expensive in Independence. She wished there'd been enough room for a great deal more supplies than they'd purchased. She knew they'd be using it now.

She'd had Mr. Henderson—she still couldn't think of him as Matthew—rest across the way while she and all the other ladies moved her belongings. She'd kept out a nightdress and a walking dress, so she could let them out. She was much leaner than she was before leaving Wisconsin, but the baby was making things too tight regardless. She could work on sewing after supper in the evenings, or during their noon breaks. The captains seemed to be allowing them fewer noon breaks in their hurry to reach Oregon City and get all the way back to Clover Creek before the snows started flying.

She thanked the other ladies for their help, and then took her dresses and mending supplies to the fire. Mr. Henderson saw her move and stood up to join her. He limped over to her without his crutches, and sank onto the ground beside her.

"Are you working on mending?" he asked. He was quite familiar with the work women did.

"I'm letting one nightdress and one day dress out. It will be better if I don't have to worry about how tight my clothes are becoming." She shook her head. "The babe grows more every day."

He nodded. "That's what they do. Did everything get moved to your satisfaction?" he asked.

She nodded. "It did. I left the small trunk with your wife's things alone, thinking you may want to go through her belongings on your own."

"There's no need. Feel free to go through them and use whatever suits your fancy. It might be nice for you to have a few more dresses."

"It might at that. Thank you." The style of dress they all wore was basically a sack. Their aprons fitted at the waist to make them look like they were fitted. That way a woman could wear a dress her entire life if she chose to. Thankfully, Jane had always had a few dresses to choose from.

As she sewed and they talked quietly beside the fire, the doctor stopped by to check on Matthew's ankle, with Betty at his side.

"It's not healing quickly, but it is healing. That's all we can ask for right now. I'd like you to keep wrapping it because it adds stability to the ankle. Without the wrap, you'd reinjure it over and over."

"What about my time on guard duty?" he asked.

"You've taken extra guard duties here and there as other men were sick or injured. Everyone is pitching in for you. Don't worry about getting back to guard duty until you're better healed than you are."

Jane smiled at Betty, one of the few women she didn't feel as if she knew well. "You and the doctor should join us for supper tomorrow night," she said softly. "It would be nice to have an opportunity to know you better."

"I have a better idea I'll talk to you about soon," Betty said. "I'm spending all my spare time learning as much as I can about medicine, so I can be a good nurse for the doctor, that sometimes even I start missing having people around me."

Jane laughed, nodding. "I don't much care to have people around me all the time, but I do like to speak to others when it's been a long while."

"The trail is much more social than I ever could have imagined," Betty said shaking her head. "I'm not sure I'll ever get used to it."

"We're over half done. You don't have to get used to it now, I don't think. You're going to want to get used to people though, because the doc will need your help once we're all settled."

"You're right about that. I've almost got all the bones of the body memorized. I'm surprised at all it takes to learn to be a nurse. I love to learn, so I'm constantly reading medical books now. It was Malcolm's idea," Betty said, gazing at her husband with a smile.

"He's a good doctor," Jane said, though truthfully, she had no way of knowing if it was true or not.

"Think about how much better he'll be with a trained nurse at his side."

Dr. Bentley laughed at that. "I don't think my worth as a doctor is changed by the nurse I have at my side. Of course, a knowledgeable nurse can do a lot for a doctor, helping him spot things he wouldn't otherwise. I suppose Betty will make me better."

Betty laughed, moving to her husband, and kissing his cheek. "You make me better every day."

After the two had wandered off, Jane wondered if they'd have ever married if not for the trail. Before she knew it, she was asking Matthew. "Do you think all of the marriages on the trail would have happened if we'd been settled somewhere?"

Matthew pursed his lips thinking about it. "Not the ones between people who were already married to other people, of course. But I think Mary Mitchell and Bob would have married. I think Mrs. Bolling and Jamie would have married. What about you?"

"I can see some of the couples marrying, but not nearly as many as have gotten married. I don't think I would have remarried quickly if I'd stayed in Wisconsin. I would have just kept teaching and my mother would have watched my baby when it was time."

"Your father wouldn't have minded?"

Jane shook her head. "No, my father died when I was young. My mother never remarried. She said she liked the freedom of being able to think for herself for a change. I can understand that, but I don't know if I'd have stayed widowed for more than a few years. There's too much living left to do it all alone."

"Do you feel like your mother does? Do you want freedom to be able to make your own decisions?"

She shrugged. "I like to make my own decisions of course, but I'm an educated woman. I read a lot, keeping up with local and world news. I don't think I would like it if a man told me how I must feel about anything. Let's take the subject of slaves for a moment. I believe a person owning another and treating them as if they were a possession is wrong. But even if slavery is outlawed in this great country of ours, will women still be slaves to their husbands? Will children still be forced to work in factories and give the money they earn to their parents? I hope not, because both of those things feel like slavery as well. Many reforms need to be made, and women aren't supposed to have opinions about them. That makes me sad."

He studied her for a moment before nodding. "I won't try to make decisions for you. If you want to discuss things with me as an equal, that's just fine by me. I will never treat you as property."

It was the same promise Adam had made Jane before they married. "Thank you. I expect to be treated as an equal, and I will share opinions as I see fit. I think that's why Adam and I did well together. He made me the same promise before we ever became engaged."

"What about the children?" he asked, eyeing her carefully. "Do you think a woman should do all the work involved in raising children? Or do you think it should be more of a give and take between husband and wife?"

"I think everything should be decided jointly. Many things the mother must decide on her own, as she's the one spending more time with the children in most cases. If it's something serious to be dealt with, the couple should have a discussion about it, out of earshot of the children."

He smiled and nodded. "We should have had this discussion before speaking our words earlier, but I'm glad we agree on the important things. And I'm glad you can cook in a way that pleases my children. I don't think I could have listened to one more complaint about how awful my beans are."

She laughed softly. "I am going to have to make beans once a week or so to keep our food supply up. I'm truly thankful that dried beans last as long as they do."

"As am I. Yes, tomorrow night would be a good night for beans. They are healthy, and the children will live. It's food in their stomachs."

"Yes, it is. And food is not exactly abundant along the trail unless we want to stop for a long period of time to hunt and gather. And then we wouldn't get to Clover Creek before the snows fell." She paused a moment. "Are you still wanting to build a hotel when we've settled?"

"I think about it a lot. It was Judy's desire for us to build it, but I would be just as happy starting a ranch. Would it bother you to be a rancher's wife instead?" Matthew truly didn't want to give up on Judy's dream, but he had to realize that with a new wife came new dreams.

"I think perhaps I would prefer to be a rancher's wife, but we could compromise. Make a house bigger than we need for our family, and I will take on boarders who come through. I can cook for them, and we will make a little extra money that way."

He nodded. "That sounds like a good idea. I know several in the group are talking about restaurants and that type of thing. In a year when the people are coming through Clover Creek, there may be a whole town there to stop and stay in if they want."

"It would be nice, wouldn't it?" Jane's gaze focused on an object off in the distance. Adam would love for her to be a rancher's wife as they'd intended. "If I'm called on to teach school, how would you feel about that?"

He shrugged. "I think it would be better if you could give the children their lessons, and they did them at home. You could just teach one day per week that way, but if you feel like you could teach a whole roomful of children every day, then you may do that. You have a mind, Jane. You may use it for whatever you please. Just make sure *our* children are taught."

Our? She was surprised by his wording of the statement, but it would be their children, she supposed. "I wouldn't let children grow up with no education."

"Are you hoping for a boy or a girl?" he asked.

Jane shrugged. "I'd like a boy who could help with the ranch work, but I'd also like a little girl with eyes like her father's." She had always loved Adam's blue eyes and thought they would be perfect on a little girl.

He nodded. "I love that you can see Judy's face in little Hattie. Not so much in Alice, though you can rarely see Alice's face with those two fingers always in her mouth."

Jane smiled. "She'll outgrow that eventually, and then we'll miss those fingers always being in her mouth."

"I have a strange feeling I'm not going to miss it at all. Her mother and I did everything we could think of to make her stop that habit, but nothing worked."

"Don't worry about it. Not yet anyway. If she's fifteen and still has her fingers in her mouth, then we'll have something to worry about."

"All right. I'll take you at your word." Matthew yawned and stretched his arms above his head. "I'm going to sleep out in the open tonight. Why don't you sleep under the wagon with David?"

Jane nodded immediately, understanding that her place was with the children. There was no doubt in her mind that's why he'd married her, but to be fair, she'd married him for mostly the same reasons. She had a baby who would be born in a few months, and that baby would need a father, and someone to support him or her. Matthew would provide that for her unborn child, even as she took care of his small children. She only hoped they would be able to coexist easily. Both were strong Christians, but that was about all they had in common. Was that enough to make a strong marriage?

Hopefully it would prove to be enough.

Chapter Six

Friday, June 16th, 1852

I married Mr. Henderson last night. He asked me yesterday morning before we started out, and I immediately said yes. What else am I to do? He proposed a marriage in name only, and that's the only kind I could have possibly agreed to. I'm still mourning Adam, and Matthew is still mourning his late wife, Judy.

I'm now the mother of David, aged seven, Hattie, aged four, and little Alice, aged three. Hattie's birthday is coming up at the end of the month, and I will try my hardest to make her feel like it's a real birthday. I can make a cake and we can invite her little friends over.

Even the children seem to be making lifelong friends on our journey. It surprises me just how well they learn to get along. Even at the end of a day when they've all walked together throughout the day, they want to play together in the evening. I certainly wish we adults had as much energy as the children do.

We should reach the lake I saw tomorrow. I haven't remembered to ask anyone the name of the lake, but it will be a good place for us to do our laundry and do a bit of hunting. I'm not sure if we will be able to take our Sunday off this week, as the captains have quickened our pace. No one is quite certain why they've quickened it, but I'm assuming they think there will be an early winter. As tired as we all get, it's important for us to be at our destination before the snows fly. None of us want to winter in Oregon City when we can be building up our settlement at Clover Creek. I pray the captains make the decisions that are right for our group of emigrants.

Jane was up and had washed before the whistle blew, and she started breakfast for her new family. The children were excited to have pancakes two days in a row, though Alice asked if they'd ever have Johnny cakes again.

"Yes, we'll have Johnny cakes a lot, but corn meal lasts longer than wheat flour. So, if we have lots of pancakes now while we can, we can save our corn meal for the Johnny cakes later on."

Alice blinked, her fingers in her mouth. But then she slowly nodded. Jane worried a bit about the little girl who rarely spoke. She hoped the child wasn't slow like so many she'd worked with.

After the dishes were finished, they yoked the oxen and got started out. Now that they had the four oxen from the Henderson family and the twenty Jane and Adam had to start their ranch, it was much easier to find oxen that were fresh and ready to pull the wagon on any given day. It should make the rest of the journey a bit easier for the Henderson family, and Jane was thrilled she could do little things to help her new husband and his children. Of course, the oxen weren't a little thing. With as expensive as they were, and as many as Jane and Adam had, it would be a perfect way to start a new ranch.

Once they were on their way for the day, Alice decided she wanted to walk alongside Jane, and Jane was perfectly fine with that. Hattie looked like she was torn between walking with the other children and walking with Jane as well, so Jane waved her on to play with the others. There was no reason for her to hold herself back and not be with the other children when she had the opportunity.

They walked along the trail and could see the Portneuf River as they walked. It was a beautiful, scenic journey, with the mountains rising majestically over the water. Jane still hadn't found the name of the lake, but that was all right. Someone would know. She was just thankful to have a map to show her what was ahead. It was much easier to tell the other women where they were going. Men didn't seem to communicate well with women geographically.

She could easily tell a woman what would come next just by glancing at a map. It was much harder to tell a man the same thing, and she had no idea why. Men and women just seemed to think very differently.

Alice seemed so happy as she walked along beside Jane, clinging to her hand. "Isn't it pretty?" Jane asked, and Alice nodded, still not removing the fingers from her mouth. She seemed to do that only to eat and speak, which was rare.

Jane found herself walking with Trudie and Penelope that day. When they once again didn't stop for lunch, Trudie asked the other two if they knew anything about why they'd suddenly picked up the pace so drastically.

"I don't think anyone is injured now," Penelope said. "Other than Mr. Henderson who is still capable of driving. I think the captains are taking advantage of that and trying to get through as much territory as we can before someone else is injured or gets sick."

"Or they're worried about an early winter," Jane said softly. She didn't want to worry the other women, because she was worrying about it enough herself, but she knew there was a good chance they'd seen signs of early winter and that was spurring them on to walk faster.

"You think?" Trudie asked. "I guess it's better than worrying bandits are on our tail."

"I can agree with that," Penelope said. "I'm going to go find the food that we had left after supper last night, and I'll take some to Herbert to eat as he drives. I may sit with him and share the meal."

"That sounds nice," Jane said. "I need to keep walking, but I'll dish up Matthew's meal and get it to the children as well. We can only walk if we can eat as well. I want to start beans soaking as well. I hate how they make me feel and soaking them does seem to help."

Trudie smiled. "I should probably go and feed Joseph and Emily. With as much energy as that child burns, I'd be surprised if she didn't fall right over if she missed the noon meal."

Jane laughed. "I understand. And my little Alice here needs her nap. Don't you, Alice?"

Alice nodded.

"I'll talk with you later," Jane said as she headed toward the wagon Matthew drove to get the food from the back where she'd stored it just in case they didn't stop for a meal again.

She was a little surprised that Trudie had been so friendly. She remembered at the beginning of the trip the girl had been downright prickly, but now, she seemed like a different person entirely. She was definitely much happier now that she was married. Jane was certain there was more to the story as there was with all of them, but she wouldn't pry. It was an unspoken rule on the trail that you didn't ask others about their past.

Jane served up five bowls of their food, first taking one to Matthew as he was the one driving and needed to keep his strength up. And then she fed Alice and put her in the back of the wagon. She found Hattie who climbed into the back of the wagon on her own and began eating. David realized people were getting food and he showed up seemingly out of nowhere to get his share of the noon meal.

As soon as all the children were eating, Jane took her own food, and fell back to walk with the other women. It was nice to have lively conversation as they walked this seemingly endless trek.

They camped that night along the Portneuf River, and before Jane even had supper ready, Trudie came and squatted beside her fire for a moment. "We're going fast because we can. The sooner we get to

Clover Creek, the more houses can be built before winter. If everyone stays healthy, we'll continue this pace. If not, we'll slow down and be thankful for having a few days we could get ahead."

Jane smiled. "Thank you! Make sure you tell Penelope."

"Oh, you know I already have. She told me to come tell you."

Jane laughed. "It's certainly nice not to keep having to guess what we're up to. How did you find out?"

"I asked Mr. Cauldron while his wife was trying to pull the boys out of a tree."

"Those boys sure do find whatever mischief there is to be found, don't they?"

"They do!" Trudie got up and hurried back to the fire that was already going at her own campsite.

Jane wished they'd do more meals as a company instead of just cooking for themselves every night. She was sure it would be easier on everyone involved, but no one really wanted to do that except for special occasions. It was one of the things she'd dreamed about before coming, and she would have loved to have a relationship with the other women that would have made it easy to do.

The beans she made that night had the children groaning loudly. "You said no more beans!" Hattie said, close to tears.

"I said I'd try not to make them too much. That's different. We haven't had any beans since I started cooking for you, and that was five days ago! That's not often at all."

Alice simply stared at her with those two fingers in her mouth.

"We can do it for one night," David said to his sisters, trying to encourage them.

"You'd think you were asking them to drink poison!" Matthew said, shaking his head. "She's going to fix a meal."

"And I'm making cornbread with the beans," she said softly. "Everything tastes better with cornbread."

Alice's lips curved up on either side of her fingers.

When the meal was ready, David took a big bite of his beans and smiled. "These beans are good! They don't taste like Pa's beans at all."

Alice pulled her fingers from her mouth. "Papa makes bad beans."

Jane bit back a laugh. "Papas aren't usually great at cooking."

"I'm glad you cook for us now, Mrs. Davies," Hattie said softly.

Jane exchanged a look with Matthew. She wasn't Mrs. Davies any longer, but what should the children call her?

Matthew seemed to understand the look. "When she married me, she stopped being Mrs. Davies and became your new mama."

"But if it makes things easier for you, you can call me Jane. That's my first name." Their father had never used it, but the children certainly could.

Matthew seemed to think about it for a moment before nodding. "I think calling her Jane would be fine."

The beans were a hit with the whole family, and Hattie even asked if they could have them again soon. Jane had added the slightest bit of brown sugar to the pot while they cooked, making them sweeter. It was the only way Adam would agree to eat beans so often, so she figured it may work with the children as well.

Once the children were asleep that night, Jane and Matthew sat near the fire, not really talking at first. Jane had no idea what to say to the man. He was her husband, but...she didn't know him. She and Adam had courted for years before they'd finally married.

Matthew cleared his throat. "I'd like to talk to you about something if I may."

"Of course!" Jane looked at him, ready to grab onto any conversational gambit he threw out. They had to talk about something.

"If I tell the children to call you 'Mama,' I would prefer you not contradict me and give them another option. I know it's easier for them to call you Jane right now, but I think they'd have made the transition easier if they called you Mama as I suggested."

"I'm sorry. I wasn't looking at that as contradicting you. I was just trying to make things easier for the children."

"I understand, and I'm not angry for that reason. If you wish to contradict me about something, please wait until we're alone, and we can talk privately."

Jane nodded, feeling thoroughly chastised. She'd thought the children were in her realm, not his. Now she felt as if she was being scolded like a child. Adam would never have spoken to her that way. "I'll do that in future. Do you need anything before I go to sleep? I'd be happy to make you another cup of coffee or something."

"No thank you. Coffee would keep me awake, and with the speed the captains have us moving, I need to sleep early."

It was just getting dark out as Jane climbed under the wagon with David, who immediately rolled toward her. The nights were cool in these mountains of Oregon. Someday she'd be happy with that cool, but that night, she was happy for the boy who snuggled close to her. It would keep her warm through the long night.

She lay for a moment awake, thinking about how Matthew had chastised her, but it didn't last long. They were just getting to know one another and learning each other's personalities. It was best if things like that came out now, before she had any real feelings for him.

Before? She wasn't sure where that word had come into her thoughts. If she ever had feelings for him, which she hoped would happen along the way. Feeling something for the gruff man who she cooked for and whose wagon she slept under seemed so far away, but she knew it could happen. She spent too much time with him for anything else to really happen.

As she drifted off to sleep, she prayed for her new family, and she prayed that feelings would develop between her and Matthew. It would feel wrong to have feelings right away, but Adam wasn't coming back, and she would need to get used to Matthew. Soon.

At least it was cool enough to sleep here, unlike how it had been when they'd first crossed the North Platte River. Now she could drift off to sleep in the fresh mountain air and feel rested when she awoke.

Matthew sat up for a while thinking about how he'd spoken to Jane, and he realized he'd been a little harsh with her. He'd never have talked to Judy that way. Perhaps he could consider the fact they barely knew one another, even though she was suddenly his wife. They needed to find the right ways to communicate about those things.

Hopefully his ankle would feel strong enough they could take a walk out into the prairie the next day. It would be better for them both if they could set some rules before they upset one another, and he could tell she'd been upset. He'd been right to tell her he hadn't liked it, but his tone of voice had been scolding. She was a modern woman, and she didn't deserve that.

Chapter Eight

Saturday, June 17th, 1852

The captains announced today that we'll be moving on tomorrow. We have had few Sundays where we were asked to skip our church service and walk. Pastor Scott said he's still going to hold church service, but he'll do it early in the morning, and those that need to do laundry can do it before breakfast. He's calling this a breakfast service because he's asking families to gather around and eat while he preaches. Then we're wasting no time.

I don't have a problem with moving on Sundays. I think it's good for us all to rest a bit, but we can skip resting one week. It won't hurt any of us.

I talked things out with Jane after snapping at her last night. It's more complicated to be married to a stranger than it was to marry someone I'd known all my life. We both have a great deal of adjusting to do.

Saturday was another day with a lot of walking. They had always averaged twenty miles per day, but now the captains were asking for twenty-five miles. It didn't sound like much different, but it was very different to Jane's aching feet.

Before they'd left for the day, Matthew pulled Jane aside and apologized for his sharpness the night before. "It's going to take some time to get used to being married to someone who isn't my Judy. I hope you won't hold it against me. I'll do my best to hold my tongue in future."

Jane smiled brightly. "I was thinking the same thing last night. Adam and I courted for years before we ever married. We knew each other so well. Now I'm married to a virtual stranger, and we will have to get used to each other in a way that may take years."

He nodded. "For now, we'll take it one day at a time. It's going to be the best for us and for the children, who are counting on us."

Jane surprised them both when she stood on tiptoe and kissed Matthew's cheek. "Thank you for being understanding with me. We'll work through it."

"Yes, we will!" Matthew smiled at his little bride. "Thank you for not being angry."

As he hurried to yoke the oxen, Jane went to find the children. Alice immediately latched onto her hand again, not saying anything. This time Hattie didn't hesitate as she ran off to walk with the other children. Jane knew they had little games they played along the way, sometimes getting themselves into mischief.

David said, "We're walking down by the water. Don't worry, I'll keep an eye on Hattie."

"All right. If you need something, don't be afraid to tell me about it." Jane smiled down at Alice, who looked so content. "We have fun walking, don't we, Alice?"

Alice nodding, a smile forming around the fingers in her mouth.

When Betty and Mrs. Cauldron walked up beside Jane and Alice, Jane smiled at them. "Are you two into mischief?"

Mrs. Cauldron laughed. "I have no energy for mischief after getting my sons out of mischief every day!"

Betty laughed. "She's not joking either. Those children will take any dare and climb any tree. One of them told me that if God hadn't meant for them to climb trees, he wouldn't have put them so close to the trail."

Jane laughed. "Sounds like a perfectly good philosophy for a young boy."

Mrs. Cauldron shook her head. "We didn't get the chance to make a fuss over your marriage to Mr. Henderson. I thought maybe we could do that tonight. There will be dancing like usual on a Saturday night, but it will end earlier. We'll make a big meal for the whole camp to share, and you'll have a night off cooking. How would that be?"

Jane smiled. "Have the other women agreed to this? Every time I've suggested we pool our food and take turns cooking, the other women tell me that's a bad idea. I love the sound of it if you can get the others to agree."

"The others have all agreed," Mrs. Cauldron said. "We even talked about making it a regular Saturday thing with the women taking turns cooking, so most can handle their family's laundry before the dance."

"That sounds wonderful to me."

"Good. We'll do it tonight then. Mary is going to try to get some game while we're walking today. Then we can use whatever she is able to shoot as our meat for the night."

"Fresh meat?" Jane asked. "My entire family is in. No one complains, but I can see the little ones getting sick of the dried meat I turn into meals. I did get them to like beans last night though. That worked out well."

"How did you do that?" Betty asked. "We all start crying when bean night comes around. We've just had our fill of them by this point."

"Adam never liked beans," Jane said. "So, before we left, knowing there would be a lot of beans on the trail, I started experimenting with them. I found that adding just a bit of brown sugar—no more than two tablespoons—to the water made them palatable for him. I got a lot of extra brown sugar to use for that purpose, and since he passed, I'm using it on the family."

Betty and Mrs. Cauldron exchanged a glance. "Do you soak them?" Mrs. Cauldron asked.

"Yes, I do, and I add the sugar to the water just as it starts to boil."

"I'm sure trying that. Soon." Betty shook her head. "It's so hard to get children to eat beans so often."

"I agree. The children had already been complaining to me about beans when I made them for the first time. They've asked to have them often. I hope it works for you."

"It seems like such a simple thing to make everyone quit complaining," Mrs. Cauldron said. "But I'll try anything at this point."

While they walked, they talked about other cooking tips for the trail. "It's hard to know what's going to be good from one week to the next," Jane said. "I wish we had food that would stay good for months on end, but there's just no way to do that. Maybe in the future there will be, but we're limited to what we have available. It seems like if there can be steam engines and photographs, someone could make food last longer without going rancid."

"I think that should be the next invention, but men come up with things to make their own lives easier. If there were a woman inventor, we'd have what we need quickly," Betty said.

"That's true..." Mrs. Cauldron pursed her lips. "My boys are certainly smart enough to invent things when they're not trying to destroy the world. I'll talk with them and get them thinking along those lines. If anything comes of it, it will be years down the road, but it's worth trying."

Betty and Jane grinned at each other. "I have no idea what those boys are going to do, but whatever it is, they're going to do it on a scale loud enough to be heard around the world. There is no doubt in my mind of that," Betty said.

"I concur!" Jane said. "We should walk together more often. I'm enjoying this conversation. Women think differently than men, and if they'd just listen to us, I think the world would be a better place."

"Oh, it would definitely be a better place," Betty said. "Thankfully Malcolm listens to my ideas. He's a good husband."

"I wish I knew if mine was a good one. I don't know him well enough yet."

Mrs. Cauldron sighed. "I'm just glad you have a father for your baby when it comes along. We don't know what kind of husband Mr. Henderson is, but we certainly know he's a good father."

Jane nodded. "I cannot complain even a little bit about how he parents his children. I hope he stays involved and doesn't just expect me to take over."

"I hope so too," Mrs. Cauldron said. "I wouldn't mind giving him my boys for a week or two. Maybe they'd act better."

"I think your boys are just too rambunctious for normal parents. They need you and Mr. Cauldron. You're the perfect parents for two boys who can't sit still to save their lives."

At lunch they once again kept walking. They were picking up five to seven miles per day by going through their noon meal and not taking a long break, but everyone was so tired. They would need a shorter day soon. Perhaps the captains would let them go for just a half day on Sunday. That would be ideal.

But as soon as they did, someone would get hurt, and they'd have to stop. Or it would rain too hard to keep going. No, it was best for everyone involved if they just kept going.

Jane got the children their noon meals and put Alice in the wagon with her sister, and then she went to the front of the wagon and climbed into the wagon seat beside her husband. "I thought we could take some time and get to know each other a little while we ate our meals."

Matthew seemed surprised but nodded. "All right. What do you want to know?"

"How did you meet your wife?" she asked.

"She lived on the next farm over. She was an orphan, and the family took her in. We met on her first day of school, and we married a few years later—as soon as we were old enough really. She was only fifteen when she had David. I sometimes wonder if she would have lived longer if we hadn't rushed things so much."

Jane frowned. "We can't look back and decide what we should have done because what we did was right at the time."

"You're probably right. I wish I'd known how soon I would lose her though. I would have tried to make her laugh more and made her feel more loved. I didn't know though."

Jane nodded. "I would have done the same. Adam was...well, he was my first and only love." Though she hoped to love Matthew someday, she didn't say that. "We were school sweethearts, and we courted for the last two years of school, and then another year before we married. He was good to me. When I wanted to teach school after we'd married, he was more than willing to let me. He thought it was good that I cared to educate myself, but he always said I wouldn't have to teach anymore once we were out west and had our ranch."

"Did you have to teach? Or did you want to teach?" He needed to know what kind of woman she was.

"For us to be able to go to Oregon sooner, I needed to. He would have been fine to have me at home and wait another couple of years, but to me, it just made sense to move to where we wanted to live as soon as possible. So, I worked. We have a nice bit of money saved for when things go wrong out west. You know they will."

Matthew smiled. "We saved enough money for the lumber we'd need for a hotel. Since we're not building a hotel, and you have a nest egg, I think we'll do just fine. Maybe I could even hire someone to help me on the ranch right away so we could have a leg up."

"That sounds really smart to me." She smiled. "I'd love to start off as we mean to go on. Get the house and barn built, and we can build anything else next summer or the summer after. I wonder if it snows a lot in Clover Creek."

"No idea. I'm sure the local Indians will be able to tell us that."

Jane frowned. "You're not afraid of Indians?"

He shook his head. "Remember how scared we all were when we left Independence about possible Indian attacks? Think of how many have died along the way, but there hasn't been one Indian attack. I think we need to start looking at Indians a different way and just trade with them, but not fear them so much."

"I'll try. I have to admit, seeing them at the soda springs scared me more than a little. I traded with them, but it just didn't seem right."

"We'll make friends with the Indians, and then our lives will be better. They have their own medicine and know how to live on the land out here. We don't. We need to learn from them."

"That makes sense," Jane said. "I'll do my very best."

"You're a good wife, Jane."

"Oh, I'm not so sure about that. All I do is mind the children and make meals. And laundry. I'll be doing your laundry."

"Do you mind that we're going to have to keep moving tomorrow? I understand the captains' reasoning, but it does seem like a long way to go with no breaks." Matthew shook his head. "I feel we should stop just to take care of all the livestock and wagons if for no other reason."

"I know that everything was in good condition when we left Clover Creek on Monday. I think that's why we stayed there so long. The animals grazed, and each wagon was looked over and repaired. We were in a good position when we left, and I'm sure we are now. I can do laundry tonight, and we'll take our breakfast to the early morning service like everyone else." Jane didn't particularly mind, but she was getting a little more tired every day.

"I guess that works. And with me driving so much, I'm certainly staying off my ankle like the doc said."

"That's true." She looked around. "I've finished eating. No use putting extra weight on the wagon. I'll walk the rest of the afternoon."

He frowned. "Do you need to ride a little more? I know you're expecting, and this kind of walk is hard on expectant mothers."

"I'm fine. I'll stay in good shape this way. Mrs. Mitchell says I'm healthy, and she expects no complications."

"Have you talked to Dr. Bentley? I'd sure feel better if he examined you and told us if you're as healthy as Mrs. Mitchell thinks you are."

"I am. But I'll see him if it makes you feel better." She started to get down out of the wagon but stopped, remembering something. "I almost forgot to tell you. Mrs. Cauldron and Mrs. Bentley are going to throw us a wedding party tonight. They're making a huge meal for everyone, and there will be dancing like there is every Saturday night. This will just be in our honor."

"I didn't say I wanted that. Why didn't you ask me?" Matthew's blood ran cold at the very thought of celebrating their loveless marriage.

"You were driving when it came up. Does it bother you?"

He simply glared at her. "Yes, it does."

Chapter Nine

Sunday, July 18th, 1852

I feel like I've wronged my husband early on in our marriage, and it seems as if he's finished with me now. I'm not quite certain what I did so wrong, but he is upset with me.

I know it has something to do with allowing the other women to cook a meal and turn our Saturday evening dance into a party celebrating our wedding, but I'm not sure why that upsets him so much. By the time he found out about it, the plan was in motion, and I didn't feel like I could go back on my agreement for the party to happen.

I hope, by being the best wife I can be, that he will finally tell me what I've done that bothers him, or even get over the fact that I agreed to it without his permission. He told me he thinks I have the right to my own thoughts and opinions so getting this angry with me over a party makes no sense to me at all.

I do hope we can reconcile for the children's sake. They don't need to watch their new mama and papa get angry with one another. Not so soon after they lost their mother. I do wish I had an idea how to make things right.

For the rest of Saturday, Matthew avoided even looking at Jane. She served him supper, and he didn't even say thank you as was his habit. She wanted to beg him to tell her what she'd done to upset him so, but he was in no mood to be spoken with about anything. He'd made that much clear.

Even when young Edna Blue danced that evening, her arms and face raised to the sky as if she was some sort of heathen, he didn't speak to her. It was odd because Edna always had tongues wagging. At one point the girl took the peppermint stick from her cleavage and pointed it at someone, but Jane was never certain who. It was an odd gesture even for Edna.

Early Sunday morning, they met for their church service, all of them with breakfasts on their laps so they didn't waste any time, and they listened to Pastor Scott talk about forgiveness.

"One of the hardest things we as Christians must do is forgive one another. Sometimes, something is done without the person who upsets you even realizing it, and if that's the case, how can you hold back your forgiveness? If I came to you and offered to reshoe your oxen, it wouldn't mean that I don't think you could do it yourself, or that you didn't have enough money to pay our blacksmith to do it. It would simply mean that I want to do something kind for you, and that would be the end of my reasoning. So many people would take slight at that when there was no slight meant."

Even though she was the one who had wronged Matthew, Jane felt as if the pastor's words were meant just for her. How was she going to be able to convince her husband that she'd meant no slight by agreeing to a party, though how he could have taken something negative from it was beyond her understanding.

Matthew never looked at her, instead staring straight ahead, holding Hattie on his lap, while she held Alice on hers.

The service was kept short, but it gave them all something to think about as the men yoked the oxen and the women did the breakfast dishes so they could be on their way. The fast pace was getting a little harder every day, but Jane wanted to be in Clover Creek before winter as much as the next person did. She wouldn't complain. Not one word.

As they started out the day, she held Alice's free hand, and they walked toward the front of the group of women. Jane liked to stay back a little further because of the dust that the oxen and wagons blew into the air, but just this once, she wasn't worried about how dirty she'd get. She was so lost in thought she didn't even notice when Hannah Scott fell into step beside her.

"Are you all right?" Hannah asked softly. "Something happened between you and Mr. Henderson. You were doing well until last night, and suddenly he stopped talking to you. How can I help?"

Jane felt tears pop into her eyes, but she blinked them away, refusing to shed a single tear over a stubborn man. Well, she didn't know Matthew well enough to know if he was stubborn yet, but he was upset and hadn't spoken to her about why, and that equaled stubborn in her mind.

"I'm not sure what happened, but I'm sure we'll be able to work things out. We're married now, and there is no choice." Jane knew some women were divorcing their husbands, but she couldn't see herself bringing that type of scandal into her life. She didn't want to forever be the divorcee.

"I'm glad you understand that marriage is sacred. Let me know when you feel like things are better between you, and if not talk to me about it in the meantime. I'm careful not to say anything to people about confidences I share with others."

Jane smiled a little at that. "You'd have to be careful being a pastor's wife and all. Do you ever feel like there's a lot of pressure on you because you are married to our pastor?"

"I do. Especially at first. I was certain every time I put a toe out of line, someone would be running to Jed and complaining. That hasn't happened though. I do my best to not sully his position in the eyes of men, but I'm not perfect by any means. I always ask him if he'd still have married me if he'd known just how imperfect I am."

"And what does he say?"

"He says he would have because I'm perfectly imperfect in his eyes. Whatever that means."

"Sometimes it's like men speak their own language, isn't it?"

"It is!" Hannah said, shaking her head. "Don't get me wrong. I love Jed, and part of him is his ministry and the way he speaks, and I won't complain about either thing. But I might *think* about complaining from time to time."

Jane grinned. "I guess you're as human as the rest of us then. I don't complain unless I absolutely must. I do wish I could figure out why Matthew is upset though."

"Have you asked him?"

"Well, I haven't. He hasn't let me speak to him since whatever I did wrong was done, so there has been no chance." An idea formed in Jane's mind. "I could get into the front of the wagon with him while I ate my noon meal again. The girls eat in the back of the wagon, and David eats with his friends. It would be very easy for me to slip away then."

"I think you should!" Hannah said. "I hate to see the two of you so unhappy when you just married this week."

"It does seem odd that he's already angry, doesn't it?"

Mary joined them then, her rifle over one shoulder. "Hello, Mary," Jane said. "Thank you for getting the elk that fed us all last night. It was much appreciated."

Mary grinned. "I do love being able to hunt as well as most of the men with us. It's good that I can be ready to shoot any game we come across while the men are busy driving."

"That's true," Jane said nodding. "I don't know what we'd all do without you. As long as you have your gun on your shoulder, I feel safe."

Mary laughed. "That's when I feel safe too. Bob doesn't seem to care for me being so self-sufficient, but he sure doesn't complain when I bring in food."

"I'm sure he doesn't!" Jane said. "You can not only hunt the meat, but you can cook it too! That's a lot more than I can do."

"I don't know how he's going to feel about me hunting when I'm nine months along, but we all know I'm going to do it. Clover Creek just seems like paradise to me. I hope no one claims the land there before we get the chance."

Hannah smiled. "I have a feeling it will be there waiting for us. Jed wants to build a church on the side of that hill at the edge of the valley. I think we'll build a parsonage on the same area of land and raise our children there."

Alice walked along with them, saying nothing, but clinging to Jane's hand as tightly as she could.

When Jane noticed the other women going to the backs of their wagons to get their noon meals, she went to the back of the wagon and pulled out food left from their meal the night before. It had been nothing short of a feast, and everyone had seemed pleased with it. Everyone but Matthew that was.

She put Alice in the back of the wagon and gave her a bowl of food. Then she found Hattie and let her crawl in herself. One of the best things about Oxen was how slowly they walked. It made it much easier to keep up with the wagons.

Jane gave David his meal, and then she fixed two last bowls, climbing into the front of the wagon with Matthew. The meal had potatoes, carrots, and elk, and it was one of the best meals they'd all eaten on the trail.

She handed Matthew his lunch before taking her first bite of her own. "This is left from the party last night," she said.

Matthew said nothing, just nodded at her as if he didn't want her to speak to him.

"I wanted to talk to you, and this seems to be the only way you'll listen to me. I want to apologize for whatever it is I've done wrong, but it would help to know what that thing was, so I could keep from repeating my mistake."

His jaw dropped as he gaped at her. "Really? You don't even know what you did wrong?"

"No, and I never will unless you tell me. I know it has something to do with the wedding party, but I have no idea what. I thought it was nice that the people we're traveling with wanted to do something for us. I couldn't tell them no!"

He shook his head. "Judy wanted a big wedding party. We decided to forgo it so we could save money to come west and start her hotel. Then I married you, a woman I barely know, and I get the wedding party Judy always wanted. You shouldn't have a better wedding party than the woman I loved!"

Jane took the verbal strike square on her chin. "I'm sorry I don't live up to your expectations. I'll continue to care for you and the children, but once we get to civilization, you should feel free to divorce me."

She got down from the wagon and ate the rest of her meal as she walked behind it. Why wasn't she good enough for him to be willing to celebrate? He had someone taking care of his children, doing the laundry, and fixing his meals. If he had no other reason to celebrate, he should have celebrated that.

For a short while, she'd believe she could eventually fall in love with the man. Now she knew better. It would be like casting her pearls before swine. And in this case, the man truly was being a pig.

Hannah caught up with her. "I guess he told you why he was angry?"

Jane nodded once. "I'm not willing to discuss it. I'm sorry."

"No, that doesn't upset me. I just think you may need to talk it out with someone."

"Do you know, I thought I could eventually fall in love with that pig of a man?"

Hannah's hand covered her mouth, and she stifled a giggle. "Well, now. A pig is he?"

"He is. You wouldn't believe what he just said to me. I'll never be good enough to even walk in his footsteps, let alone sleep on a pillow his real wife's head has touched. I went into our marriage with an open mind. I knew I'd be better off with protection, and I could help his family a great deal. But did he give me the same kind of chance I gave him?" Jane kicked a rock that was in the middle of the trail.

"I guess he didn't give you a chance at all. But tell me something, Jane. When you look at him, do you compare him to Matthew in your head? Can you really say that your late husband is no longer in your heart?"

Jane glared at her friend. "Well, of course he's still in my heart. Matthew must have a tiny heart though, because it's apparently completely full of his Judy, and there isn't a speck of room for me or any other woman. I just want to kick him."

"Did you tell him that's how you feel?"

"No, of course not. After he said what he did, I got down from the wagon seat and came back here to stew. Your husband sure picked a bad week for a sermon on forgiveness, because I can't seem to find any forgiveness inside of me after what he said."

Hannah smiled. "Then he picked the right week. His topics aren't always comfortable with people, but they are useful. It might be time for you to climb right back up on that wagon seat and tell him how you feel about what he said to you. If he doesn't know why you're upset, how can he correct things? You need to forgive him and move on. Wouldn't Adam want you to be happy in your new marriage?"

"Adam? No, he'd have wanted me to stay married to his memory for the rest of my life!" Jane said.

"Really? I know if something were to happen to Jed, he'd want me to remarry and move on. Especially if I was expecting."

Jane sighed. "Yes, he'd want me to remarry, if only for the sake of the baby. Why do you have to be so practical?"

"I think I started being practical when I married Jed. It just came with the job."

"And being married to the pastor is a chore?" Jane asked.

Hannah shrugged. "At times. Anything can be a chore you know. I don't mind going for walks, but here we are, having walked since the beginning of March. Of course, I'm tired of walking and it's become a chore."

"You think I should go tell him how he made me feel and forgive him? Really?"

"Well, you haven't told me what he said, but I think I've put the pieces together. Yes, you need to go and talk to him and forgive him. Do you know why?"

Jane shook her head. "No, but I'm certain you're about to tell me."

"Because forgiving him will remove the anger from your heart. It's good for you, not him."

"I hate it when people are right when I'm being angry."

Hannah laughed. "Don't we all?"

Chapter Ten

After calming down some, Jane joined Matthew on the wagon seat again. She sat beside him, staring straight ahead for a minute, and then she spoke. "I'm sorry I didn't understand how you felt about the wedding party. It didn't occur to me it would bother you." She took a deep breath. "You hurt my feelings by telling me that I'm not as good as Judy, and don't deserve more than she had. I know those weren't your exact words, but that's how they hit me. And it hurt. I married you because I needed help, and I knew you did as well. And because I can see a future for us. I can see myself falling in love with a man like you. But I forgive you for hurting me. And I know I am falling in love with you a little more each day. If you don't want to stay married to me, then you can do something about it once we've reached our destination. I can fall back on teaching as I planned to do when Adam first died."

Matthew couldn't look at her. "I think that's what bothered me so much about celebrating our wedding. I knew I was already in love with you. You've been kind and loving to my children, and you've put up with my orneriness a time or two. I believe that we could have a good marriage if we were both to work at it."

"I believe we could as well. My baby will only know you for its father." Jane waited to see how Matthew would respond, but she didn't dare look at him for fear he'd have a mean look on his face again.

When Matthew spoke, it was quiet, and his hand covered hers. "I'm not ready for a real marriage with you yet. There's too much guilt inside me for Judy's death. I know you'll tell me it wasn't my fault, but if I hadn't wanted to make her dream a reality by moving west and having a great deal of land to build on, then she wouldn't have died. She wanted a hotel back east. I'm the one who insisted on heading west."

He shook his head. "I'm sorry that I've taken out some of my guilt on you. I don't mean to make you feel badly about yourself or about our marriage."

"Does this mean you've forgiven me?" she asked, her voice hopeful.

"There's nothing to forgive. I am the one who reacted inappropriately, not you. You did what you should have done. You came to me, talked to me about the problem, and then forgave me before I could even think about what it was you had to forgive. I'm not worthy of a woman like you, Jane."

"You are. I understand guilt. What if I had just asked him to stay back east one more time? Would he have agreed? What if I'd been able to convince him to wait one more year to come west? Would he have survived the crossing?"

He sighed. "I guess you really do understand how I'm feeling about it all. It's funny how we blame ourselves for the deaths of our loved ones, isn't it? Wouldn't it be better if we could just understand that it was their time to go? Perhaps there was a reason they needed to die just then. Perhaps there wasn't. All I know is that I need to stop kicking myself, so I can learn to stop kicking you."

Jane bit her lip, nodding. "I'm willing to work toward having a good marriage with you. Perhaps we can spend a little time courting when we get to Clover Creek or right here on the trail? We skipped that part of our relationship, and I don't think it's done us any good."

Matthew wrapped his arm around her shoulders. "I'm determined to make our marriage work. We'll start courting just as soon as we can. Thank you for giving me another chance to treat you as I should." He turned and kissed her cheek, just as she was turning to kiss his.

Their lips met for the first time ever, and it felt...right. There were no fireworks like there had been with Adam, but there was comfort and security in his kiss.

That evening, as she was cooking supper for her new family, Matthew walked up behind Jane and tapped her on the shoulder. She turned to see him with his hair combed and a bouquet of flowers in his hand. He hadn't even combed his hair for their wedding. He'd let himself go after Judy's death.

"What's this?" she asked, grinning up at him.

"I thought I'd ask if you wanted to go for a walk after supper tonight. Mrs. Scott offered to watch the children, and I think it would be good for us to learn what courting would be like between us."

"I would love to go for a walk with you after supper!" she said, surprised to see him holding the flowers and following up on the talk they'd had earlier.

"What is for supper, anyway?" he asked.

"I cut up some of the jerky I had, and I made a gravy with the pieces of the meat in it. And I'm making a large pot of potatoes that we'll eat the gravy over. And now that I know it's a special courting night, I'll put some biscuits on."

He chuckled. "You don't have to go to extra work. You've already caught me."

She laughed. "I don't have to, but I want to. Let me put the flowers in some water, and then I'll start the biscuits. I'm sure the children will be thrilled to have bread with their meal."

He sat beside her on the ground, watching her movements at the fire. Judy had never felt comfortable cooking at a fire, but Jane seemed to have been doing it all her life. Each meal she made was better than the last. "The children don't care what you make as long as I'm not the one cooking for them."

"From what David said, your beans were pretty bad..."

He chuckled. "One time I burnt them onto the pot, and when I tried to clean it, I couldn't get them all the way out. So, I kept cooking beans in the same burnt pot, and the children hated it. I finally got the pot clean, but by then, the children hated my cooking and complained no matter what I made."

She laughed. "I think it's good they know their father doesn't walk on water. Some children never learn that."

"Mine know it well. And they're still young!" He looked down at the flowers he still held in his hands. "Does Alice still cling to you during the day?"

Jane nodded. "Until she's eating her noon meal, I'm not allowed out of her sight. It makes her feel better to know that I'm always where she can reach me. She doesn't really talk much, she just clings to my hand and sucks on her fingers."

"I'm thankful she's taken to you as she has. When Judy first died, she seemed to want to climb into my skin with me. It's only been the last month or so it's been a little better, and now with you, she doesn't seem to care about me at all. And when we're stopped for the night, she plays with the other children. I don't know how much she remembers."

"I think I'll be the only mother she remembers. It's sad because I know Judy loved the three of them as much as she loved her own life. But it'll also be good because she won't have memories of her death. Hattie might, and David definitely will. I think we may have some problems with the two of them down the road."

"We may. But we'll get through it all together. We married so we each had someone to lean on. Let's lean on each other." Matthew looked down at her for a moment before brushing his lips against hers for the first time on purpose. "Thank you for forgiving me, whether I deserved it or not."

"I'm happy you are in my life. Imagine if I'd had to marry someone like George Bedwell! I'd have been poisoning that man's coffee every morning."

He threw his head back and laughed, realizing only then that it was his first real laugh since Judy died. "You're very good for me and my children."

"And you give me someone to lean on so I'm not constantly worried about what will happen to me and my unborn child."

"We'll talk after supper." He got up and wandered away, and she noticed that he was barely limping. Jane couldn't help but be pleased to see him walking around and doing well.

Matthew was true to his word. As soon as she finished the dishes, he led her down toward the river. "I thought the river was a more romantic place than anywhere else, and you're getting romance."

Jane grinned at him. "I'm not sure I need all that much romance. I've been married before and have a child on the way."

"You want courting, and with courting, comes romance. So, you're getting romance. I'm sorry I can't quote Shakespeare or any poetry to you. I should be able to, but I just didn't pay attention to things like that in school. I can read, write, and do arithmetic, but when it comes to poetry, I completely ignored that part of my schooling."

She laughed. "I remember some, but I don't think any of it needs to be quoted for a proper courtship. Just take me on walks and tell me I don't look like I swallowed a watermelon whole, and I'll be happy."

He shook his head. "I can't even tell you're expecting, so don't worry about looking like you swallowed a watermelon whole. I don't know how much walking you're going to want to do after these long days we're having." He walked to a boulder and sat down on it, motioning for her to sit beside him.

"I don't know how much walking I'm going to be wanting to do either. These last days have been grueling. I do hope we can stop this next Sunday for a full day. I'm not sure how many more days I can go with no noon break and no days off." She leaned against him as she reached down and massaged one of her calves.

"Do you need to ride with me?" he asked, looking at her with concern.

"Not at all. I do well walking, but I'm tired. I should be. The children are well-behaved and it's as easy for me as it's going to get."

Matthew sighed. "Keep eating your noon meal with me. That's been nice when we aren't fighting."

"But that's all we do when I ride with you!" she said, grinning at him.

"Well, from now on, when I start being difficult and you want to kick me, kiss me instead. It will keep us from fighting."

"I might try that."

"You should probably practice. Make sure you know just the right way to get me to keep quiet."

Jane laughed, but she raised her lips to his obediently. "I think we're getting the hang of it," she said after a long silence.

"I think we are." He looked down at his hands for a moment. "I can't promise I won't turn into a grizzly bear at times and say things I shouldn't, but I can tell you that I'm falling in love with you. I want you to stay my wife no matter where we end up, and I want to raise your child as one of my own."

"I'd like all that as well."

"Then we're allowed to argue a little, but we'll have to kiss as soon as either of us starts to get upset. It may not seem like the right time to kiss, but it'll be better for our marriage than anything else could be."

Jane nodded emphatically. "You're right. We just have to both agree that when we start getting upset, we'll kiss. It's that simple."

"I'm agreeing now. And I plan to have you in my bed...soon. Not today. Probably not even next week or next month. But perhaps when we're settled into our little house in Clover Creek, we'll make our marriage a real one."

"That sounds like the best plan we could possibly have, doesn't it?"

Sunday, August first, 1852

I have to admit that being married to Matthew hasn't always been easy, but we're learning to talk to one another about everything that matters. Alice is still clingy with me, but it's nice to be loved by someone so completely.

It took a while, but I can now happily say that I'm completely in love with my husband, and I'm happy that we're together. It won't always be roses, but my marriage to Adam wasn't perfect either. He had a temper, and I riled him up at times. Usually when I was disagreeing with him about the practice of slavery, but I'll not waste ink on that.

David seems to have accepted that I'm his new mother, and both Hattie and Alice call me Mama now. David still calls me Jane, but I don't mind that one little bit. He's the one who spent the most time with his real mother, and I think he'll take longer to completely warm up to me.

I feel as if we have the right foundation, and I love that he still asks me to dance every week, and he tells me I'm beautiful. He's learning to not be afraid to love me as he was at first, which is good, considering how very much I love him.

This long trek to Oregon is difficult, but I wouldn't change it for the world. It brought me a new family and so many good friends. I feel like I finally have the sisters I wanted when I was young.

Life is better than it was a month ago, and I believe it will continue to get better the further down the road to Oregon City we go. And then home. To Clover Creek.

Oh, I almost forgot. That lake I was looking forward to? It's really just where the Snake and Portneuf Rivers come together.. Nothing terribly exciting after all.

Note from the author:

Now that everyone is safe in Clover Creek, there are still so many stories to write about the people from the wagon train, and others that will come along.

I've decided to start a new series called *Clover Creek Community*. I plan on the first book coming out on September ninth. The first story will be about Jared and Emma and will be called *Emma's Engagement*.

Thanks for following me through the series. I've done extensive research on the Oregon Trail and it was so fun to bring people to life this way. I hope you'll follow on and watch what our pioneers do from here.

If you want to be notified when I have a new book out, please text Bob to 42828.

Thanks again, and love to all!